FATED TO THE FORBIDDEN

Serena Blackthorn

contents

CHAPTER 1

"And why wasn't I told about this sooner?" I growled with barely contained rage.

The maid shrank back in fear, but she answered. "I-I just f-found out a-about it."

I cursed loudly and slammed my fist into the wall. "Dismissed."

She ran away, and for that, I couldn't blame her. If I were in her shoes, I would do exactly that. Run.

After all, I was a VERY mad she-wolf, and I wouldn't think twice about harming anyone in my way.

I stormed downstairs and when I couldn't find anyone, I sprinted to the pack house. I didn't bother shifting because it would take too long, and I wanted answers immediately. Finally, I reached the door that led to my father's study.

I threw the door open and came face to face with the Alpha of our pack.

Aka, my dad.

"What the hell were you thinking?!" I yelled. He looked up from his desk and merely raised an eyebrow. He knew better than to interrupt. Instead, he let me rant for a full minute.

"I can't believe it! This is the Broken Ash pack we are talking about here, correct? We are enemies! You just don't accept their word that all they want to do is have a party to find the Alpha of that pack a mate, do you?!? It's a trap! The Alpha of that pack is said to not even have a heart, and you think he is coming through here with his most important and strong pack members just to find a mate?!?! No sir! I see right through this little plan, but do you? Noooo. The Alpha is not coming through our land and inspecting all the girls of age in our pack to find a mate, Dad! He is going to try to kill us!"

Finally, my father seemed to get annoyed by my rant and he stood up.

"Enough."

Instantly, I shut up.

He continued, voice sympathetic but stern. "Adira, you are quite an extraordinary she-wolf. You can outrun anyone in the pack excluding me, you can fight dirty and well, you win at everything you do, but your one weakness is your own imagination, and the refusal to see a temporary surrender when it pops up. You don't have your mate. You of all people I thought would have understood this. You must trust the Alpha of your pack. I will make sure you are safe and not harmed. Would I do anything that would intentionally harm you?"

Mutely, I shook my head.

"No, I would not. The Broken Ash pack will be arriving tomorrow at late afternoon. All the unmated females within age will go to the feast that is being prepared. The Alpha will join them at the feast and see if he can find his mate. If he doesn't, he leaves. If he does, he takes her home and that's that."

I sighed, nodding. "I'm sorry."

He smiled softly. "It's alright honey. Just try not to jump to such rash conclusions, yes?"

I smiled, about to hug him, but what came out of his mouth next caused me to freeze.

"And you will also have to understand that you could potentially be his mate. You are, after all, unmated and 19 years of age, which is a little late. Your brother has his mate already and he is a year younger than you."

I swallowed the unladylike words that were trying to force its way out through my lips. Instead, I offered him a tight-lipped smile. "Of course. I'll be on the training grounds if you need me."

He sat down and gave a nod of his head, and I breathed a small sigh of relief.

I had been dismissed.

I watched the rink and the fighters inside. The once before friends now looked at each other and circle the other, wary. A determination was written on both of their faces, and they both were in fighting stance.

"Begin." The judge said, and instantly they started to fight, punching and kicking and ducking. For five minutes, they play fair and hard, and when the five minutes is up, the judge speaks again. "Time. Mr. Hart, you win because you had Mr. Que in the most positions that would have counted against him had this been a real match. Good job, boys. Who's next?"

Nobody raised their hand, and I knew why. The next round was going to be a match. That meant that unless the other player surrendered, you weren't getting out of that rink.

Knowing I needed to let off a little steam, I stepped up onto the platform. The judge and our teacher raised an eyebrow but didn't say anything to me. Instead, he addressed the gathering crowd as a whole.

"Who is willing to fight Ms. Adira Dame, daughter of the Alpha of the Moonhigh Pack?"

Silence.

Just like I expected, honestly. I probably looked ready to scrap, and knew nobody would be brave enough to try to fight me if they were in their right minds-

"I will."

I turned towards the male voice and sighed. Of course, it just had to be Xavier. Well, like I said before, nobody in their right mind would fight me. He is obviously not in his right mind.

I grinned evilly though and accepted.

Did it matter that he made it clear he wanted me as his mate? Did it matter that the attraction he felt for me was nothing because I hated him for trying to get us to get a mate bond already?

No. At least, not right now. I needed a good match, and he was a good fighter, so I knew he would give me a good fight.

We both entered the rink and wore similar smirks. I knew both of us were doing this for much more than to just blow off steam. We wanted to prove to the other the strength we possessed. I mind linked him before we started.

When you see how strong I am, and when I win, that will prove to you that I don't need a mate.

He answered smoothly. When I win, it will prove to you that you need me.

"You may begin." The judge said, worry evident in his voice. Our hands were wrapped in gauze, indicating to everyone that we would not go down without a fight.

Xavier looked me dead in the eye. He looked almost sorry, but I looked further into the depths of his hazel eyes and saw triumph. He thought he had won already.

Ha! I would show him.

I lashed out with my foot, but he jumped high in the air and lashed out with his own in a quick kick towards my face. I caught his foot and twisted, and he fell to the mat with a groan.

I was about to pin him to the mat when he suddenly leaped up and swung his fist around. I barely avoided it, the air whooshing past my face as if to mock me.

I growled and circled him.

He did the same, and then we both got serious. He came at me with a series of punches. One of them caught me on the side of my jaw, and I knew it would leave an ugly looking bruise later. I yelled and lunged for his legs, bringing him to his knees.

I managed to kick him in the side solidly before he rolled away and grabbed my hair, yanking it back. His hand encircled my throat, but I grabbed his other arm and brought it down with all my force, causing him to cry out. I smiled viciously and crouched before jumping up and advancing on him with a series of roundhouses. One of my kicks hit right between his legs and he fell to the ground in pain.

I only felt a little guilty for fighting dirty, but then I thought of why I was fighting and who I was fighting, and my resolve hardened. I kneed him in the chest, and then quickly straddled him.

Pressing my arm to his neck hard, I hissed a breathless,"Surrender. You're beaten."

He whispered,"I will never submit to you. And no, I'm not beaten. It's called a distraction."

Before I could figure out what he meant, I was thrown off with a simple hip maneuver. I let out a surprised yelp and then suddenly he was on top of me. His knee pressed into my chest, and his hands gripped my hair and yanked backward, forcing my neck to be exposed.

"Submit." He growled. I met his eyes with a glare and was surprised to see that they had turned black.

I swallowed and watched his eyes follow the movement before I opened my mouth and whispered an answer.

"What?" He said, brows furrowed. He leaned in, putting his face closer to mine to hear me.

Perfect.

With a burst of strength, I brought my head up to his with a loud crack, my hair giving a painful rip, and with a cry he released me. I pinned him down and held a claw that had unintentionally grown against his throat.

Xavier froze, eyes locked on mine.

"I've got you, Xavier." I breathed, and when he made a move I pressed tighter, not enough to draw blood but to let him know I wouldn't hesitate to do so.

He seemed to be having a battle. Just as he was about to surrender, I heard my dad yelling. Uh oh. He knew where I was.

"ADIRA SABRINA DAME!" The Alpha roared, and I leaped off Xavier as if just being near him burned me. I waved my hand at Xavier,"Go! He might not punish you if he didn't know you wanted to fight me!"

Instead, Xavier came up and put an arm around my tense body just as the Alpha came into view.

He saw us, the spectators around the rink, and growled. "My office. Now."

He spun around and stalked to the pack office. I sighed angrily, shrugged off Xavier's arm, and followed.

"Explain."

All three of us sat around my father's desk, and from the look on his face, he was angry.

I let out a frustrated groan and clenched my fists. "I've already explained a thousand times! I was pissed went to the fighting rink to let off some steam. Nobody but Xavier would fight me, and you caught us just as he was about to surrender."

Through all of this, Xavier hadn't said a word. Of course, it's when I say this is when he decides to speak up.

"Actually, the last part is incorrect. I was about to throw her off using a special maneuver my father taught me, but she got off of me before I could get a chance to."

I whipped my head and gaped at him in astonishment.

"What?" I looked at him with angry incredulity. "That's not what happened at all!"

Xavier clenches his jaw before speaking again. "Yes, it is."

In a fit of anger, I rose out of my seat to finish what we started but Alpha Dame spoke voice calm.

"Stay seated."

I sat.

"Adira, what you did was not right. When you are angry, you absolutely do not challenge others to a fight. That was not how you were raised."

I bowed my head. "Yes, papa."

He turned to Xavier, and I tensed, waiting to see what he would say. "You, young man, are brave, yet foolish. You have a smart mouth on you, yet you also have natural instincts that would make you fit to be a leader. You have many disadvantages and advantages at your disposal. Know what they are and how to use them, because one day you may find yourself at the end of a rope with no way to go but down, and when you fall, it will be what softens it that counts. Both dismissed."

I sighed and stood up, deflated. I'm not sure what I expected, but it wasn't that. I always knew Xavier was dad's favorite, but in all honesty, it was getting old.

"Adira."

I paused on my way out the door and watched my father stand up. "The reason I called you is because there has been a change of plans. The feast has been bumped to tonight, at 7:00 on the dot. I expect to see you there prompt and on time. Do I make myself clear?"

I sighed and knew I wouldn't be able to argue. "Crystal clear."

He gave me a firm nod. "Good. And that situation with Xavier..."

He trailed off and I suddenly found myself afraid of what he was about to say next. However, he just shook his head and grinned, suddenly amused. "Don't worry, I believe you."

"Huh?" A great response, I know.

"Xavier's a good fighter, but not as good as you. I have no doubt in my mind that he was ready to surrender before I called your name. I'm sorry I couldn't have called it a minute later."

I laughed, shaking my head in agreement. "Me too. I think it's about time to take him off his high horse."

Alpha Dame nodded in agreement. Suddenly, his eyes glazed over and I knew he was mind-linking someone in the pack. When he came to, his brow was furrowed and his mouth was set in a hard line. I saw the worry in his eyes and grew concerned.

"What's wrong?" I asked, stepping closer.

His face took on a blank slate quality and he brushed past me. "Nothing for you to worry about. Now go and get ready."

He left, already in mid-shift.

I frowned, tempted to follow him. Though he might've forgotten something trivial like a regular meet with the Beta, I had a feeling that wasn't the case. It had to be something more significant. The question was, would I be able to see what it was without being caught?

My mind was made up when I peeked out the still open door and saw him disappear into the woods. I shed my clothes in less than a second and chased after him, careful not to draw too much attention to myself. I made sure I was running lightly on the ground and didn't make noise or leave footprints.

I focused my breathing and picked up his scent, which wasn't hard considering he was the Alpha. I slowed to a jog and then a simple walk when I heard voices up ahead.

"...absolutely not. She's only 19." I heard my father's voice, and then another voice laughed.

It was a rough, hard voice and it made me shiver in disgust. "Only 19? Do you hear yourself, James? Most girls have their mates by now. Most get theirs when they turn 18, and from what I also hear, she's soon to turn 20. That's two full years of being mateless, chump."

They had to be talking about me. Who else would they be talking about? My suspicions were confirmed when my dad spoke up in a firm voice.

"Let's get one thing straight, Omega. You do not refer to me as 'Chump,' you will call me Alpha Dame. Secondly, who are you to focus this conversation on my daughter? This is not why I came here, and if you do not give me the information I need, I will not hesitate to call in my pack warriors and turn you in as a Rouge."

The raspy-voiced Omega laughed again. "Sir, yes sir. Getting right down to business, I see. You'll be able to pick it up at..."

He paused, and I heard him sniffing the air. "Someone's here." He growled, and I didn't pause to think.

I just ran.

I ignored their shouts and snarls, instead focusing on losing them. Right now wasn't the time to be worrying about what my father was involved in. Right now was the time to outrun the Alpha of my pack.

I heard them gaining behind me and knew I might have to risk going off our territory if it meant losing them. Hopefully, that wouldn't have to happen.

I took a sharp left and saw the river coming up about 50 yards to my right. I headed for it, knowing once I passed through it my scent would be temporarily masked and I would be able to easily cover my tracks.

The water was cold but I forged onwards and kept running, ever so subtly veering back towards the pack house.

20 minutes later and I crept under my window, dripping wet. In my haste to get away, one of my paws slipped on a rock in the river and I fell. It was probably for the best, seeing as I was able to quickly lose them after that.

I shifted and hastily pulled on a flowing dress and gym shorts that were hiding in the bushes right under my window. I was always prepared and had clothes spotted at strategic locations.

Never knew when I meet need it. Right now was a prime example.

I climbed the tree and jumped, catching myself on the ledge that jutted out and swung myself onto my balcony. I crept inside and leaned against my wall with my eyes closed, then finally let myself breath a sigh of relief.

"Where were you?"

Alpha Dame stood in the middle of my room, arms crossed. Shit.

Chapter 2

I climbed the tree and jumped, catching myself on the ledge that jutted out and swung myself onto my balcony. I crept inside and leaned against my wall with my eyes closed, then finally let myself breath a sigh of relief.

"Where were you?"

Alpha Dame stood in the middle of my room, arms crossed. Shit.

"Oh. Hi Dad! And how are you this lovely evening?" I asked brightly, making sure to keep a smile on my face.

"I would be better if you told me where you just were." He told me with a dead-panned face, and I knew I would have to bring some major charm into this conversation if I was getting out of here alive.

"Would you? Well, that's just great, because I was just about to tell you! After you left, I decided to go on a run. Somehow I wound up in the woods and I passed through the stream. I slipped. I fell. I ran back. And here I am!" I spread my arms, grinning like a fool.

His eyes narrowed. "You're not telling me everything."

Damn, he's good. I need to step up my game.

"Yes, I am. What else do you need to hear?"

He gave me the stink eye and I sighed like I was finally giving up my secret. I hung my head slightly for effect and let my mouth have a mind of its own.

"I was hungry and wanted a teeny tiny snack because you know how my appetite is, it's unquenchable! So I caught a bunny and ate it, guts and blood and all, and it was very, very, very delicious. But then you want to know what happened? A whole family of bunnies just ran away right in front of me and so I chased after them-"

"Enough." He barked, and I smirked.

"What? You wanted details. Do you want more? I happened to feel very queasy after that, and then-"

"Get ready for the dinner tonight, Adira. You have an hour." He left my room, slamming the door on his way out.

I let out a breath and ran over, locking it. Did he seriously just fall for that? I tend to ramble when I lie, and I knew that was turning into a full-on monologue.

I shuddered at the thought but applauded myself for quick thinking.

Now I just needed to get ready for tonight.

As I drew a bath, my mind wandered to the idea of having a mate. Was I against it? No, I don't think so. At the same time, though, it depends on who the person I'm mated to is.

I instantly thought about what was to happen in an hour, and who was trying to find himself a mate. The Alpha of the Broken Ash pack. I involuntarily clenched my teeth, and my hands curled into fists. I've heard so many stories about him, stories that aren't at all pleasant. He's the kind of man that momma's told their kids stories about at night so they wouldn't get out of bed.

He's the kind of man that killed just for the fun of it, the kind of man that enjoyed torturing rogues. Alpha Phoenix didn't have a good bone in his body. I even heard that he was the one that killed his father so that he could become Alpha quicker.

His pack was merciless and ruthless just like their leader. I felt so sorry for whoever was going to be his mate. I really hoped it was no one from our pack, since our pack is known to be very gentle and caring, and at times spineless.

However, those traits didn't apply to me, my father, or my mother. We are known for our iron fists, and we make sure that this pack is run smoothly, with the help of the Beta's of course.

I always stood up for what I believed to be right, even to the point of fighting. I had been training ever since I was a little girl and liked to think I was very skilled. In fact, to give the training teacher of the Pack Warriors a break every once in awhile, I decided to train them. I knew that I was better than even Alpha Dame, but I held myself back.

I held myself back in a lot of things.

Without my permission, my mind flitted back to what happened 2 years ago.

"Mercy!" My mother yelled voice panicked. I was too entranced with what lay in front of me to pay much attention.

We were in the woods, right before a huge grassy clearing. It was night time, and there was a full moon that night. It was cloudless, so the stars shone bright, not that it would have mattered. My eyesight already allowed me to see perfectly during nighttime.

A large white wolf lay directly in front of me. Its fur was matted with dirt and caked with blood, some still fresh and dark red. Its eyes were half closed, and out of its mouth came the most awful sound. A heartbreaking whimpering escaped, and I rushed to his side. I was in human form, and I wasn't thinking very clearly.

The only thing that kept going through my mind was 'I have to try to save him, or at least give him some comfort in his pain-induced state that he was currently in.'

So I did. He didn't fight it when I placed my hands on either side of his wounded face and blew on him. My limbs seemed to have a mind of its own, and only instinct kept me going. Incredibly, I could see my cool breath travel down the wolf's body. As it did so, the wounds and dirt and blood all disappeared, as if it was never there.

This type of power had only been mentioned in the old legends of "Rhaknorisk." It was said that a strong female wolf had the power to heal someone or something fully with only a exhale of air onto the wound. It not only healed them, but also gave them rejuvenation. They were left with more life in them than ever before. And only one female wolf had that power a long, long time ago. Her name was Lilia. Lilia was appointed the powers by the Moon Goddess herself, so she was extremely special.

How was it that I even knew how to do that? I didn't know what came over me when I approached the White Wolf and just blew on it. It was like someone had taken control of my body and I sat in the back of mind, watching through somebody else's eyes.

The Wolf blinked and raised its head into the air, almost as if he couldn't believe what had just happened. His coat was a startling white, almost too bright to look at directly. And his eyes- absolutely gorgeous violet eyes.

I heard the sound of distant paws hitting the ground at a fast rate and knew they were looking for this wolf. My mother finally reached me and yanked on my arm, pulling me up and off the ground where I was kneeling. "We have to go NOW!" She yelled and I turned towards the wolf one last night.

He was on all four paws and was staring at me with unblinking purple eyes.

"I will remember you." I heard a deep male voice in my mind before my mother screamed," Shift and run after me!"

I shifted and ran after her, not caring that my clothes ripped. I snatched them in my jaws and sprinted after her. We were able to make it away safely, but my mom made me swear not to tell anybody about what had happened that night. Nothing, especially the part about my newfound powers.

I never did. Even to this day, it was a secret me and my mother kept close to our hearts. Not even my father knew, and though it was at times hard to hide it from him, it was for the best. We didn't know what it meant, and so we would keep them hidden. This is why I was a better fighter, a faster runner, and a stronger wolf in general. At least, that's what my Mom and I guessed.

More questions arose, as they did every time I thought about that particular night. How had that White Wolf spoken to me in my mind? Unless I imagined it, which I knew I didn't, it shouldn't have been possible.

But then again, I was apparently just like Lilia, and we didn't know the full extent of her abilities. She was, after all, just a legend.

A banging on the door made me jump and a voice yelled," Open up! You've got .1 seconds!"

It was Trish. I grinned and sped to the door, opening it as fast as I possibly could. I stared at her hair, which was now in front of her face from the force of the wind that the door swinging open produced, and she blinked.

"I didn't mean literally." She complained, shoving past me and going straight to the bathroom. She emerged with my favorite brush and promptly started brushing her hair so it was perfectly straight again. Her dark golden locks fell in a straight line down her back and barely above her butt.

She had been growing it out for as long as I could remember and I guessed it paid off. My own hair length wasn't too shabby. It ended in the middle of my back platinum blonde, almost white waves. I only went to get it trimmed once every 3 months, while she got the dead ends trimmed once every 6 months. Most of the time I just put my hair in boxer braids, so they wouldn't get in the way.

One look at the determined set to Trish's face and I knew she was going to style my hair any way she wanted and I would get no say in it. However, when she took a deep breath before opening her mouth I knew she was going to go on a rant.

"I heard we are going to a feast in 45 MINUTES. I REPEAT 45 MINUTES. That is not enough to do everything I have planned for you! Why didn't Alpha Dame tell me sooner? Why didn't you tell me sooner? In fact, why didn't you tell me, period? You know how long it takes me to get ready for these kinds of things. It will take me at least an hour to figure out what I'm going to wear and what makeup to put on. And we're showing off for Alpha Phoenix, no less! I heard he's the sexiest looking male on the face of the earth, and if that's true then not even 2 HOURS will be enough time to look steaming-hot, stunningly gorgeous-"

"Jesus, Trish." I interrupted, shaking my head in amusement. "With you chatting like that you just wasted another 2 minutes. Shut your pretty mouth and just get yourself ready! I'll do my own makeup, and you can do my hair after your done. Got it? And remember, you're already beautiful without makeup, so don't go overboard or else it might detract from your natural beauty."

She frowned but nodded and I brushed past her to get my makeup brushes. I wasn't trying to impress anybody, so why bother dressing up? I knew my dad and mom would want me to, though, so I kept the lip stain, lip liner, and mascara.

I rummaged through my closet to find a dress but knew it was going to be a tough find. I usually just wore t-shirts and shorts, even in the winter. For some reason, I was always uncomfortably warm, so I never wore jeans.

I couldn't find a dress so when I asked Trish, she was happy to oblige. "I've got one that would fit you perfectly!"

She then giggled. I kid you not, she fucking giggled and ran from the room, a comb still dangling from her hair. Sometimes I question her sanity. Then again, I question mine all the time so I shouldn't judge too harshly.

In less than 10 seconds she ran back with a dress in hand. The minute I saw it I shook my head. "I'm not going out in the presence of unmated werewolves with that dress, Trish."

She stood in front of the long mirror and held the dress flush with her body. "Why not? It's cute."

I snatched the dress from her and held it at arm's length. "It's strapless, backless, and ends higher than mid-thigh. I would wear this to a strip club, not some dinner where our enemy is playing nice with us."

She mumbled something under her breath so low not even I could hear it before taking the dress back and exiting the room once more. I noticed she still hadn't removed the comb from her hair and decided to tell her that when she came in again.

This time she entered the room with three dresses in tow, and the comb was out of her hair. "Here. These should fit your approval, your highness."

I stuck out my tongue and took the dresses. One was a dark red dress that was flowy, with a neckline that would show some cleavage but not too much. The other was black and ended above my knees. The neckline was pretty moderate, but the dress was tight and would definitely show off my curves. The last dress was a light blue with a sweetheart neckline and no back.

I went to the bathroom and tried the first one on, then came out and showed it to Trish. She smiled. "Me likey. Go try the next one on."

I put on the black dress and looked in the mirror of the bathroom and instantly fell in love. My curves were prominent, and my legs seemed to go on for forever, despite the fact I was only 5'4. I stepped out of the bathroom and Trish's mouth fell open. "Oh my god, yes. Yes. You are going to wear that, I'm making you."

I chuckled. "I love it too, you won't have to force me to wear it. Do you still want to see how the blue dress looks on me?"

She shrugged. "Why not."

I did so, and it looked pretty but not as good as the black dress did. Trish agreed and we settled on the second one. Since we took more time picking the dress than we thought we would, we both opted for a simple dark-lip-long-lash makeup look and left our hair stick straight, with the help of the flat iron.

When we were done, we had 5 minutes left. "You look gorgeous!" I complimented Trish, meaning every word. Her gold colored hair went beautifully with the first dress I tried on, which she decided to wear.

"So do you." She clapped her hands, excited. "What if I find my mate tonight?"

"Then I would feel sorry for you. This is the Broken Ash Pack we're talking about." I commented, and she sighed before nodding in agreement.

"It's just, I turned 18 six months ago and still haven't found a mate..." She trailed off when she realized who she was saying that to. "Shit, I'm sorry. I didn't mean to bring that up-"

"It's fine." I gave her a tight-lipped smile and opened the door. "Ladies first."

She went through and I followed, almost running into my younger brother, who happened to pass by my room. His eyes widened when he saw me, and then he grinned. "Sexy. I like it."

I gasped and hit his arm and he pulled away, laughing. "You don't say that type of stuff to your sister!"

He smirked. "Just did."

I huffed and glared at him, but a smile found it's way on my face when I saw him meeting up with his mate, Lissa. She was super sweet, and I'm glad at least he found his mate and was happy. His face lit up when he saw her and he kissed her quickly on the lips. She blushed at the audience and hugged him, burying her face in his shoulder.

"Awww." Trish cooed before rushing past them after looking at the clock hanging in the hallway. "Crap Crap Crap!" We both chanted as we tried to sprint in our flats without them falling off. We had less than a minute when we reached the special Packhouse reserved for such occasions as this.

When we entered, my eyes fell on all the unmated girls. They were chattering and whispering excitedly, oblivious to the fact that we were just to eat side by side with the same pack that had surely killed some of our own. One of them pointed to where my father stood talking to our Beta, and I nodded my head in acknowledgment.

When we reached him, he stopped talking and his eyes lit up. "You both look so beautiful tonight."

Both me and Trish replied with gracious," Thank you's."

Alpha Dame checked his phone and then put it away into his back pocket. "Their here." His eyes glazed and I heard him mind-link those in attendance.

Be on your best behavior. You know what I expect from you, so don't disappoint me.

All the girls immediately straightened their backs and fixed their hair one last time before the doors swung open. With it, the most delicious scent entered the room. Oranges and vanilla filled the air around me and I inhaled, not seeming to get enough of it.

Alpha Phoenix stalked in, and he looked every bit as dangerous as I was led to believe. Tattoos covered what bare skin I could see. He had dark brown hair, the sharpest jaw I had ever seen, and a perfect nose. His eyes were a violet color, and when they locked onto mine I knew without a shred of doubt what he was going to say before he said it.

"Mate."

CHAPTER 3

Alpha Phoenix stalked in, and he looked every bit as dangerous as I was led to believe. Tattoos covered what bare skin I could see. He had dark brown hair, the sharpest jaw I had ever seen, and a perfect nose. His eyes were a violet color, and when they locked onto mine I knew without a shred of doubt what he was going to say before he said it.

"Mate."

I stared at him in disbelief. No. This couldn't be happening. He was a monster.

He ignored all of my fellow pack members and headed straight for me, his stride determined. I subtly shook my head and took a step back. This wasn't real. This was a dream, a nightmare-

"My daughter is your mate?" My father stood taller and looked at him, a steely look in his eye. Alpha Phoenix stopped in front of us and didn't spare me a glance as he answered. "Yes."

Even though I didn't want him as a mate, I felt a pain in my chest when he disregarded me as though I were nothing. However, this only strengthened my resolve when I said I didn't want him. I hadn't told Trish or anyone else, but I had already packed a bag to leave if it came to that, and I had a growing fear it would most definitely come to that. Alpha Phoenix didn't seem the type of man to let go of his mate easily, but I was as stubborn as a mule.

I refused to go with him.

My father looked at me and then back at him. "Is this true, Adira?"

On the outside, his voice was calm and collected but I could hear the underlying trace of panic. I shook my head. "No."

The lie tasted bitter on my tongue, but I had no other choice. Alpha Phoenix's eyes pierced mine and he clenched his jaw, nostrils flaring.

"What did you just say?" He asked, voice deathly quiet.

I gulped but held my ground. I lifted my chin and squared my shoulders. "You're not my mate."

Without warning, he took both wrists in his hands. I gasped as shocks traveled up and down my arm and he smirked with dark amusement. "You were saying?"

I tried to break free but he tightened his hold. I ignored the other tingles and glared at him. "Your hands were cold. It startled me, that's all."

My father took a step forward, eyes flashing yellow, a sign that his wolf was going to come out. "Adira says that you're not her mate and I believe her. Now get your hands off my daughter."

Alpha Phoenix tilted his head. "Adira. What a lovely name."

I held back the shiver that threatened to give me away. I had to get these emotions under control or else I would find myself in the hands of this killer. "My Mother gave it to me."

I heard a few snickers at the sarcastic response, but I ignored them as my brow furrowed. Where was my mom, anyways? She should be here. In fact, I hadn't seen her all of today or yesterday, which was unusual.

I bit my lip as I thought and a growl brought me back to the present. Alpha Phoenix stared at my lips. His eyes were dark, a sign of lust.

Alright, that's it. I yanked with all my strength and managed to break free, though from the pain raking down my arms, I knew his nails would leave scratches. I didn't bother checking, my pulse racing.

I turned around and shoved past my dad, then proceeded to run to the back of the house. I heard my mate shouting orders but I focused on sprinting as fast as I had ever dared to before. I had to get out of here. I swerved into a branching hallway and ran upstairs. I shoved the guest bedroom door open and pulled the window open with vigor, almost breaking it in the process.

I swung both legs over the sill and jumped, pushing my body outwards. I grabbed onto the protruding branch from the large oak tree and lowered myself onto the ground. I then proceeded to sprint all the way to the pack house, my feet barely touching the ground. I heard some of the Broken Ash pack members running after me, but I pulled ahead easily. I swerved every once in a while to try to get them off my back, since some of them were too close for comfort. I didn't know where Alpha Phoenix was and it worried me, but I didn't have time to dwell on it.

I made it to my house in less than a minute and ran upstairs, my breathing ragged. I had stashed my to-go bag under some dirty clothes in my hamper, which was right next to the door. That was so it was quick and easy to grab. As soon as I opened the door, I froze.

A figure stood with his back to me, facing my balcony. Orange and Vanilla pervaded my senses and I stiffened. How had he found my room? How did he get here before me, period? I hadn't held myself back when I ran, and I knew I went super super fast, faster than any werewolf I knew.

Alpha Phoenix turned around and faced me, his hands in his pockets. "My wolf doesn't like that you're disobeying me." His eyes shone in the near darkness, and I worked hard to control my breathing. This wasn't supposed to happen. I should have been able to grab my bag and go, not have a mate who was faster than even me and beat me to my own room.

I sneered at him. "And I don't like that you are being a conceited ass."

As soon as I said it, I knew it was a mistake. I was only speaking my mind, but that didn't go over well with Alpha Phoenix.

"Repeat what you just said, I dare you." He growled. I must have had a death wish because I spoke up to comply.

"Well, you asked for it. I don't like that you are being a conceited a-"

Without warning, he rushed towards me and pinned me to the wall with my wrists held above me. I groaned as pain flared down my arms and head, and felt something trickling down my arms.

"Little mate, I am only once going to say this. You do not disobey me. Everything I say is final, and you will respect that. Do you understand?"

"You're hurting me." Is all I replied, my eyes filling with unshed tears. Why did the Moon-Goddess pair us up? What did I do that was so awful? Okay, maybe I took 20 dollars from my Dad, but that was only because my favorite perfume was on clearance and it was usually 50 bucks.

Instantly, he backed away, eyes wide. I stared at my arms and winced. There were deep gouges down them, and they were open and bleeding freely. For some reason, I don't heal as fast as normal werewolves do, so when I get an injury I usually don't tell anyone, lest they find out my secret.

Alpha Phoenix moved towards me and I shrank into the wall. He didn't stop, instead taking my arms in his and closing his eyes.

What the f-

A burning sensation traveled through my hands to my shoulders and down the length of my body. I opened my mouth to scream but he was there, pressing his hand on my mouth to ensure no sound escaped. When the burning stopped, he leaned in and whispered into my ear," Let me make a deal. If you look at your arms and they are injured still, you don't have to come back to my pack. If they are completely healed, you do."

"Deal." I croaked back. No way, after that pain I just felt, could I suddenly be healed. We didn't own those types of abilities: At least, normal werewolves didn't. He took a few steps away to give me some much needed space.

I looked down and couldn't believe it. I was healed. Completely. Even the scars that were on my forearms disappeared, which had gotten there from a Rogue attack a year ago.

"How?" Is all I could whisper.

His face was stone cold, and he once again turned back to the dangerous Alpha. "Questions weren't apart of the deal. In two days time I'm coming to get you. That should be enough time to pack and say goodbye to your friends and family. And if you're not still here in two days, your family will suffer the consequences."

With that, he vanished.

Punch.

Alpha Phoenix was my mate.

Spin, duck, slice, punch-punch-punch.

I was leaving my home in a day to live with a monster.

Back-flip, punch, kick, spin around and stab.

He healed me, which shouldn't have been possible since we didn't even complete the mate bond yet. And even then, he only should have been able to speed up the process, not completely heal me.

Kick, slash, duck, punch-punch-punch-roundhouse-kick, front flip, punch.

"Whoah, easy there, tiger. What's got you in a mood?" Xavier strolled up to the dummy I was beating up and stood behind it, holding it still while I let out my frustration.

"Whats got you thinking I'm in a mood?" I asked breathlessly between hits, causing him to ground his feet more firmly so he wouldn't budge backwards.

He peered at me behind the dummy and shook his head. "I've known you since we were babies, so don't pull that. Go ahead: spill."

This was usually the part where I would tell him to bug off and I would go and find Trish or someone else to talk to. But right now, Trish was in training class and wouldn't be out for another two hours, and I needed to talk to someone about the situation. Or at least, tell them about Alpha Phoenix being my mate. I may not have liked Xavier, since he was too cocky and full of himself, but I knew he was a good listener and kept secrets close.

We used to be best of friends, back in the day before he turned 18, before he found out his mate was a Rogue. Ever since then, he had wanted me as his, and though I felt awful about what happened, I couldn't bring myself to say yes. After all, my own mate was out there, waiting to find me. Now that I actually had my mate and knew what type of person he was, I wondered if things would have been different if I'd agreed to get the mate bond with Xavier.

I stepped back and unwrapped my hands, walking over to the bench that held my towel and water bottle. I sat down and wiped my face, then took a swig from the bottle. Xavier, determined, sat next to me.

"C'mon, Princess. Just for me?" He pleaded, and I grabbed his hand in mine.

"Swear you won't tell." I said forcefully, staring him in the eyes.

His brow furrowed but he squeezed my hand and nodded. "I swear."

"Alpha Phoenix is my mate."

I said this quietly so only he could hear, and I could tell he did because he reared back in surprise.

"Wait, what? But the pack just left without any explanation at all-"

"Be quiet and let me explain." I cut him off, then went on to tell him everything that had happened last night through private mind link so no one would be able to hear.

When I was done, his hazel eyes were dark with anger. "When he comes back here I'm going to make sure he doesn't leave alive-"

"Xavier!" I hissed, pulling him back down onto the seat. In his anger he had stood up, and I wasn't looking for a fight.

"I don't know how to tell my family. That's why I haven't told anybody yet, except you." I explained, looking down at my fingernails.

A hand went under my chin and lifted my head up so I was looking at him. "We'll tell them together. Would that be alright with you?"

Shocked at his offer, I could only hug him. "Thank you." I whispered with gratitude.

He smiled and pulled me up beside him as we walked to the pack house where I knew my father was. My younger brother should be there too, and so should my mother.

The instant we walked into the house I could tell something was wrong. Voices drifted from the living room, and I followed the sound with Xavier in tow. We hadn't let go of each other's hands, but I found it comforting. As soon as I saw who was inside the room, I let go of his hand but it was too late.

Alpha Phoenix narrowed in on our hands and a second later, Xavier was on the ground and Phoenix was on top, throwing punches.

"Stop!" I yelled, rushing towards them. My mate didn't listen, his hands a blur. I took a deep breath and pushed him as hard as I could. Taken off guard, he flew off and hit the wall.

I gasped at my strength, but my family's attention was on Xavier, who had stood up and was already healing. He sped over and stood in front of me, and the look in his eyes screamed 'Don't mess with me."

Alpha Phoenix slowly stood up and turned his attention to me. "Who is this." He growled, demanding an answer.

"Just a friend." I answered truthfully, and when his shoulders relaxed I knew he believed me.

"Good. But he shouldn't have been touching you." He clenched his hands but I held out my hand, fingers spread.

"We were just holding hands, nothing for you to worry about. Now, onto more pressing matters." I glared at him as I asked this next question. "What are you doing here? I've still got another day to tell them and get ready."

He raised an eyebrow. "You haven't told them yet?"

Before I could justify myself, he laughed, and it wasn't a re-assuring sound. "Don't worry, petite fille. I already told them that you were confused and scared, and didn't know we were mates. I also mentioned that we came to an understanding that now we are both perfectly clear in the fact that we are mates."

"That's not what I wanted an answer to. I wanted to know why you're here. You said I would have two days to get ready before you came. Unless you dropped out of elementary school and don't know basic math, you would know it's only been one day."

My mother gasped, and I remembered we had an audience. We were in the living room of the pack house, and mother, father, and brother sat on the three separate chairs. By the way they looked at me, they were all mad and though I couldn't blame them, I also couldn't help but feel like they should understand.

My mate was the Alpha of the Broken Ash Pack, for good-ness sake! That's not something I'm just going to casually drop into the conversation.

"A situation came up." Phoenix vaguely explained, not seeming bothered by my blatant disrespect.

He turned to the Alpha of this pack and asked the one thing I dreaded hearing the answer to. "Do I have your permission to take my mate back to my pack?"

I held my breath, waiting for the answer. Please say no please say no please say no-

"Yes." Came my father's pained reply.

I gaped at him, astonished. He wouldn't look me in the eye, and when I looked at my other two remaining members of my family, they wouldn't look at me either.

"Unbelievable." I fumed, not able to comprehend what was happening. My whole plan was for my dad to say no when Alpha Phoenix asked permission, and then my mate wouldn't have any say about it. But guess what? My dad said yes, even after knowing what type of person my mate was. In fact, most of the horrible stories I heard about Alpha Phoenix was from my father! And then he just goes ahead and says yes, ruining my only chance at happiness?

No. He doesn't have the right to do that. I am my own she wolf, I can make my own choices. And if my mate doesn't like those choices, than too bad.

I rushed out of the room, ignoring the sudden shouts of my family, the loudest coming from my father. I tuned them out and ran straight for the forest, not really knowing where I was going or what I was doing but knowing that I wanted to get as far away from there as possible.

Orange and vanilla invaded my senses and I couldn't help the good feeling that came over me when I smelt it. It was an amazing scent, a scent that I could spend days smelling and wouldn't be able to get enough.

My thoughts must have gotten me distracted, because the next thing I knew I was on the ground with my face in the dirt, a heavyweight pinning me down. "Get off me," I grunted, surprised when I realized I was still in my human form. Why hadn't I shifted?

"Not until you promise not to run." An answering voice said above. I grit my teeth and managed a small shake of my head. "Not happening." I ground out.

I tried moving but his knees were on either side on my body. He lay on his forearms down the length of my back. Tingles erupted down my body and I sucked in a breath, hating the mate bond.

"Why don't you want me?" He asked, his lips grazing the shell of my ear.

To keep from answering the question and to get him off of me, I said," Fine, I promise not to run. Just get off me, you're crushing my spleen."

He chuckled, climbing off of me. "Do you even know where your spleen is?"

I huffed and proceeded to get up, rolling my eyes. "Not the point. The point is, I don't want you on top of me unless I..." I trailed off, seeing his eyes turn dark.

"Crap," I muttered, and he took a step closer to me until we were so close my chest was brushing up against his. I stared up at him, cursing my shortness. It wasn't usual for a werewolf to be only 5'4, but then again, since when was anything about me normal?

"Don't say stuff like that unless you want to be marked and taken right then." Phoenix stared at my lips and I licked them, playing with fire.

"Sir yes sir." I replied quietly, not taking my eyes off of him.
*****

Since I've had these chapters pre-written before deciding to put it up on Wattpad, I've been updating at a faster rate than I normally would.

Thanks to everyone who is reading, and comment, vote, and follow!

~White-Rabbit

3,203 words

I was the one who looked away first.

"I've got to finish packing, since I thought you wouldn't be here for another day."

Alpha Phoenix closed his eyes and breathed deeply, seeming to control himself. I waited, and my eyes had a mind of their own and started looking over his tattoos. What did they mean? I wondered if there were any more underneath his clothes.

The instant my mind went there, a flush rose on my cheeks and I willed myself to think of something, anything, else. I heard a throat clear and my eyes snapped to his, his violet gaze piercing mine, his mouth lifted in a smirk. "What are you thinking, little mate?" He asked, taking a step towards me.

My face grew hotter but I innocently shrugged. "Unicorns. You?"

Phoenix's smirk grew dangerous and his eyes dark. "Do you really want to know the answer to that question?"

I lifted my chin. "I mean, I asked you what you were think-ing. I think it would be common courtesy to reply and rude not to answer."

He took another step forward. "I was thinking about how I would love to fu-"

"ADIRAAAA!" My brother yelled, cutting off whatever Alpha Phoenix had been about to say, and I was glad. I'm sure by now my face looked like a tomato and that was not a pleasant sight. Not that I cared how he thought I looked or anything.

I sighed before answering through mindlink. "I'm coming."

On the walk back I was silent, and Alpha Phoenix was quiet too. It let me have some time with my thoughts. My mate at times could be abrupt, but he wasn't as bad as I was led to believe. He did cut me, but that was when I tried and failed to run away. However, things might change when we went back to his Pack. Hopefully he wouldn't be totally possessive like most, ok all, Alpha mates were.

My mind went back to Xavier and I winced. Yeah, definite-ly possessive. When I went to protect Xavier, I thought that when I went to shove Phoenix it would be just light enough to get his attention onto me and off Xavier, not make him fly across the room and hit the wall. I knew Werewolves had strength, but I threw a flippin Alpha across the room with just a push.

And the funny thing was, nobody even seemed to notice.

Maybe it had something to do with me being able to heal with just a simple breath. Just thinking about it made me nervous, so I stopped thinking and just walked. In no time it seemed, we were back at the pack house.

My eyes shuttered, I turned to Alpha Phoenix. "Let me say good-bye to them right now. Alone."

Even before I finished talking he was growling. "You could try and escape again, or do some funny business with Xavier. No, I'm coming in with you."

I growled in response. He may have been an Alpha, but I was also an Alpha's daughter and didn't take orders. "No you're not. You're going to stay right here until I come out."

Phoenix's hands shot out and gripped my wrists and I resisted the urge to roll my eyes. Not this again. "You will do as I say. Do you understand?" His eyes were starting to flash, a sign of his wolf coming out.

I felt my own canines lengthen and glared at him, challenging him. "Oh, I understand perfectly well."

I saw him smirk before saying the second half of my statement. "But that doesn't mean I will obey."

I could see him getting angrier with every passing second I was talking, but I had to make him understand where I stood in our relationship. I wouldn't let myself be bossed and ordered around like some servant. If I was to become his Luna, then I would make sure I was treated with respect and treated as his equal.

"I am not your servant, Phoenix. I expect to be treated like your equal. If I am to be your Luna, then I will need to be a strong Luna to protect the pack. If something happened to you, I would need to be able to hold my own and have the respect of neighboring packs. I need to strike fear and awe in

Rogues, and in the pack. I refuse to be seen as some weakling that trembles at your touch."

Throughout my entire speech, his hands were growing tighter and tighter on my wrists until I physically felt them start to dislocate. "And get your damn hands off of me, you're going to break my wrists."

He let go as if I had burned him, but there was still plenty of fire in his eyes. "You dare tell me what to do, mate? I am your superior, your leader, your Alpha. I can and will do anything I fucking please, and I will make sure you learn your place. I'm not going to deal with your shit. You're just my whore-"

That's it. I was not just his mate, I had a name. And did he just call me a whore? This man needed to be taught a lesson.

I reeled back and slapped him with all of my strength. His head whipped to the side and his hand flew to his cheek. His eyes were wide, as if he couldn't believe that his mate would dare defy him and actually stand up for what she believed.

Before he could fully react, my brother, Braxton ran out of the Pack house with a panicked face. "There's a Rogue attack. Follow me now!"

He left as soon as he came, heading towards the woods we had just come out of. I went to follow him, fuming from my fight with Alpha Phoenix and ready to beat up some Rogues, when a hand shot out and yanked me back.

Not expecting it, I let out a startled shriek. Phoenix glared at me. "You're not going, you're staying here."

"The hell I'm staying here!" I shot back, pissed. "You don't tell me what to do, mister."

He growled. "Stay here and keep yourself safe, or else." With that, he shifted and ran after Braxton, not sending me a backwards glance. That bastard! I would show him.

I shifted and followed with fast pursuit, almost on his tail. I heard the fight before I saw it. Growls, snarls, and barks filled the air, as well as yelps and shrieks of pain. I could only hope those shrieks of pain were coming from the Rogues and not my pack.

As soon as I neared the brawl, I stopped and quickly assessed the situation. Two black Rogue wolves surrounded one of my Pack Warriors. The Pack Warrior snarled at the two wolves and abruptly attacked the one on his left, sinking his teeth into its throat. It struggled but to no avail: It was dead in a few seconds. The other Rogue was on top of the warrior in a split second, and the warrior flung the dead rogue away and clamped on the oncoming wolf around his leg. The Rogue howled and managed to bite the pack warrior, but then the Rogue was attacked and killed from behind by Braxton.

"There's three more." I heard my father mindlink me and my brother, and we locked eyes. He was on the other side of the clearing, and he looked very angry.

Shit.

I ignored him and focused on what was happening at hand, which happened to be a Rogue coming straight at me.

A huge Midnight black wolf leaped over me and sank his jaws into the Rogue's neck, instantly killing it. The wolf turned and locked eyes with me, snarling. I growled back, tensing for a fight but stopped when I noticed the violet eyes. It was Phoenix.

He growled at me and gave me a look that I knew meant he would deal with me later. If I was here when he decided to 'deal with me later' was still to be decided.

Two more Rogues suddenly attacked and Phoenix growled at them. They slinked around, circling each other. The next thing I knew, all the wolves were rolling around on the ground, just a blur. I couldn't discern one from the other, and struggled to see who had the upper hand. In a minute, the Midnight wolf with violet eyes stood up from the carnage. The other two-

I looked away. I could deal with blood and guts, sure, but only when necessary. I didn't need to see the Rogues in the state they were right now. Their throats were completely ripped out, as were their stomachs. All I could see was muscle, blood, and bone.

My stomach heaved at the sheer brutality of the act and I fought to keep my breakfast down.

After a few more minutes, my father had finished patrolling the area and came back, his eyes a dangerous black.

Meet me at the Pack House in 10 minutes.

He left in a flash, and everybody obeyed and followed after him except one other wolf beside me: Alpha Phoenix.

He suddenly shifted, then went around a tree and found some shorts. I took this opportunity to shift, changing as well. When he came out from behind the tree, my eyes widened. Tattoos covered his entire torso. Some were just designs, so I could clearly see the 8 pack he sported, and others disappeared down his v line, and I forced my eyes back up.

He didn't seem to notice, instead looking off in the distance, his eyes glazed.

He soon snapped out of it and focused his gaze on me. I peered closer, not believing my eyes. His purple eyes shone with...was that fucking amusement?

"You passed," Phoenix smirked.

My mouth dropped open and I couldn't speak for what had to be at least 10 seconds. "What?" I finally managed to say, and he full out laughed.

His head tipped back and his mouth broke into a true, open-mouthed smile. This time I was speechless for a whole other reason: He was unbelievably gorgeous. When he smiled, his whole face lit up and he seemed a lot less intimidating.

When Phoenix finally stopped laughing, he looked straight into my eyes. "It was a test."

I was still confused, but then a horrible explanation came to mind. "Wait, you planned the Rogue attack?!"

His eyebrows raised and he shook his head quickly.

"No, the Rogue attack was not planned. I'm talking about me acting like a jerk. To throw your words back at you. I acted like a 'conceited ass' to see what your reaction would be. I needed a strong Luna that would stand up for what she believed in, a strong Luna that would protect the pack from other packs and Rogues: And me."

At this, his eyes flicked away from mine. "You're perfect. You stand up for what you know is right. Don't worry, I will be sure to treat you as my equal and to not treat you like some lowly servant. "

He added with fervor, "And you aren't my whore."

It took me all of point five seconds to comprehend this. When I did, I was outraged. "What, so I'm just a toy you can play with? Oh, let's act like a fucking ass and see how our mate responds? Is that what you were thinking, huh?"

My hands were moving around like crazy. I was so mad at him I couldn't even put it in words to describe how angry I was, so I did my best which may or may not have consisted of curse words. "You fucking bastard! I'm done being played by you! Other girls might like it when you act all possessive and cruel and play them but I don't. So go find yourself another mate from all of the girls you've fuc-"

Phoenix shot at me, and I didn't even blink before I was pinned to a tree, my wrists pinned over my head, his body so close to mine I couldn't even think about escaping.

He then held both of my wrists with one hand, squeezing them together so I couldn't break free, and held the other firmly against my mouth so I couldn't talk. "You will listen to me right now, and you will listen closely."

Phoenix was so close I could see the flecks of silver in his eyes. "You were gifted to me by the Moon Goddess, yes, but I will not tolerate the way you are speaking to me."

I moved my mouth, trying to tell him I didn't like the way he was treating me, but he wasn't finished. "You are not some 'toy,' or some plaything, alright? You are precious to me. The whole reason I made the test was to make sure you were strong just like I had heard you were."

At this, my face formed a confused look. "Heard you were?" Is what I tried to say, but it came out as," Er ooh er?"

Phoenix seemed to know what I had wanted clarification on, so he went on to explain. "I know you've probably heard lots of stories about me, and none of them good. But let me tell you, I've also heard stories about you. I heard you were fierce and strong. I've heard you're stubborn and never give up for what you believe in, and that you're a fast runner, even faster than your Father. I've also heard you have an amazing talent at healing."

I froze, holding my breath. Did he somehow know? When he went on to explain, I relaxed. "You are always in the pack Hospital taking care of those who need help."

"But I'm not sure how true all of those things are." He went on to say, his eyes boring into mine.

"I'm not as cruel and harsh as you may have heard. There are these things called rumors, and people do tend to stretch the truth when telling stories. That being said, I didn't know what type of mate you were. I needed someone who stood up for her rights and wasn't some weak minded Luna. I need you to give me a chance, Adira. Please."

He took his hand away from my mouth, presumably to let me talk, so I did.

"Why did you hurt me then? If it was all presumably just an act."

At this, Phoenix's eyes filled with guilt and he ran a hand through his hair. "I had to make it seem believable to get a true reaction out of you. I'm so sorry. I will do whatever it takes to make it up to you, but for now I will have to settle with asking for forgiveness."

Wow. That was not what I was expecting whatsoever. However, I would take this over a controlling and cruel mate any day. If I was being honest with myself, I had to admit it was certainly an effective way to see what I stood for. It did have it's flaws, though. What if I had been so stubborn I rejected him the night he told me that he was taking me away in two days? And when he mentioned I had probably heard lots of stories about him, what did he mean by that?

I asked him to explain himself. "In the beginning, you said I had probably heard lots of stories about you, and not all of them nice. But you also mentioned that there are a lot of rumors and lies out there. What I want to know is, what is true?"

He chuckled without amusement. "You're going to have to be more specific than that." He said, and I swallowed before asking the question I wasn't sure I was ready to have answered.

"Is it true you killed your father?"

CHAPTER 5

He was silent for a minute. That minute turned into two minutes, and longer. Finally, I couldn't take it anymore. "Phoenix?" I said softly, my eyes searching his. They were cold and emotionless, so different from what I had just seen.

His grip tightened, and I couldn't help but wince. He didn't notice, or just didn't care. "You will not ever mention my father again." He was using his Alpha tone, leaving me no choice to obey him. Even if he hadn't used his Alpha tone, I would have obeyed.

I simply nodded.

His grip loosened, but he didn't let go. Phoenix murmured," Thank you," then put his nose in the crook of my neck, breathing deeply. I stilled, uncomfortable. I wasn't use to being shown affection. Even my mother was sometimes cold and distant, so different than most think.

Phoenix chuckled, pulling away. "Your scent calms me, love."

I looked away from his burning gaze, uncomfortable. "That's nice." I muttered, and he stepped back, chuckling.

I raised an eyebrow at this man's antics. I swear, he was bipolar.

"Let's go back to the pack house." I said quickly, heading away from the cursed tree, leading the way. He fell into step beside me, not talking. We made it back to the pack house in less than a minute and judging by the raised voices inside, they started without us.

"Alright, I'll go in first and then you can go in-" I started planning, my finger moving in the air, but Phoenix walked right past me ignoring what I was saying.

"Hey!" I jogged to catch up, my cheeks flushed at being so blatantly disregarded. "Listen, my father is probably going to be really mad and I think it would be best if we didn't go in together so he wouldn't be reminded of us being mates. Because us being mates makes him mad and he's already mad, so.."

When Phoenix turned around and stopped, his stance wide, I realized I was rambling and shut my mouth. He always seemed to bring the worst out in me, and I had to reign in my emotions.

"Why would us being mates make him mad?" He asked, his voice soft but deadly.

My already heated cheeks turned into a raging inferno when I realized my mistake. "What? Pssht." I made a face and waved my hand, trying to play it off. "No-o! What?! Who said that? I didn't say that, did you say that? Or are you asking me-"

"You're rambling." Phoenix mused, the corner of his mouth lifting in a smirk.

Again? I groaned and covered my face with my hands, embarrassed. He came over to me and drew my face into his chest, where I hid my blushing face gratefully. It seemed my slip up of how my father felt about Phoenix was forgotten-for now. Hopefully, it would stay off the table and not brought up again.

Glass shattered inside the Pack House and I peeled away from my mates chest and started forward, my stride focused. When my father grew out of control, which unfortunately with his temper happened quite often, I was the only one able to quell it, along with my mom. Although sometimes not even she would be able to get him level headed. I wasn't afraid to take a few hits if it meant the safety of our pack. It hasn't come to that since a couple months ago, though, so praying to the moon goddess it stays that way.

Phoenix grabbed my wrist and spun me around, and my cheek pressed up against the very chest I had just escaped. "Where do you thing you're going?"

"Um, into my house, maybe? You know, where the breaking glass is?" As if to prove my point, more breaking glass resounded through the house.

"It's not safe for you." His eyes looked troubled but I rolled mine.

"I've done this thing before, he's usually fine after-" I bit my lip, almost giving up one of my secrets. That was too close. Was the mate bond really affecting me this much? I would need to keep a closer guard on my words.

"After what?" If I thought he simply looked 'troubled' before, right now he was outright furious.

"Nothing, just let me go." I replied, yanking free. I ran to the door before he could protest and kicked it open, storming inside. My father stood on the other side of the room, breathing heavy with a broken vase in his hand. My mother stood tentatively in front of him, her hands out. One was bleeding freely, and I felt anger rise within me. Xavier stood next to my brother, his face unreadable. My brother was standing in front of the couch, shoulders tense. His voice was as authoritative as I've ever heard it.

"You need to calm down and think about what you're doing." Braxton ordered, his eyes narrowed. I looked from him to my father. Alpha Dame had the most enraged expression on his face. If I was being honest, he looked off his rocker. I had never seen his this way, and I was afraid for what caused it.

"Alpha Dame." I said firmly, and all three pairs of eyes swung my way. They looked grateful, and I gave a slight nod to show them I would deal with him. My mother backed away and I took her place, though my hands were down at my side.

I wouldn't show weakness. I faintly heard the door open, signaling my mate's arrival, but I ignored him. I looked into my father's crazed eyes. "Why are you mad?" I asked, my tone soft.

"Don't treat me like a child." He growled at me.

I growled back," Then stop acting like one."

He threw the piece of glass at me and I dodged it, bending backwards so far my head almost brushed the ground. I straightened and took a step forward. "Why the hell are you so angry!"

"It's none of your goddamn business-"

"It sure as hell is! I'm a part of this pack and it is my job to keep it safe. From you." I added, and by the shocked look on his face I got through to him. Sometimes his wolf took over and you had to use harsh words and actions to get him in his right mind again.

"What is the meaning of this?" Alpha Phoenix suddenly appeared by my side.

I tried to wave him away, but it was to no avail. Phoenix shouldered his way between me and my father. "You are being a disgrace to your pack and family."

I had enough: I was also afraid that my father and mate would start fighting. I always had to deal with my father's temper growing up. I learned quickly how to deal with it in a quick and efficient manner. That was the only way that his anger would diffuse.

"I'm not going to ask you again. Why are you mad? And if you don't want to give me an answer, than I don't want to deal with all of this." I waved a hand in his general direction.

He ran a hand over his face and then jerked his head in the direction of his office. I knew without him saying anything what he was implying at. I trailed behind him and then, for what had to be the 100th time, I was yanked back by Phoenix's strong hand.

"What are you doing?" He asked, though it sounded like a demand. A demand that sounded a lot like 'stay here and let me deal with him.' But that wouldn't get to the bottom of things, and dad's mood swings were unpredictable.

"Look, I was fine before you came along. No offense." I added, a sigh escaping. I found it too much work tip-toeing around my father and his moods, but now I have to do it with Phoenix too? I continued my mini speech with a tired but determined facade."But point made, I've already dealt with this and more before. So please just let me do my thing and get to the bottom of this."

My mate gave one nod, and I flung myself at him, wrapping my arms around his torso and squeezing like I used to do when I was a kid. "Thank you." I said breathlessly, then raced to catch up with Alpha Dame.

I didn't get to see his expression, but I wasn't sure I wanted to.

I met my father in his office. He was sitting in his chair with his head in his hands, looking completely distraught. I softly closed the door behind me, careful to not make any sudden moves that might set him off.

He looked at me, his eyes bloodshot. His hair suddenly seemed a lot more grey than brown, and the wrinkles seemed more prominent. "I don't know what's wrong with me." Was the thing that came out of his mouth. That sentence alone sounded broken. My breath caught and I looked helplessly at my hands. Was I really the best person for this?

My father continued, not at all like the strong Alpha I had always seen. "My temper gets out of control and my wolf takes advantage of that. Did you see my wife in there? I made her bleed. I wanted to make you bleed. Even those first turned manage to control their wolves within the first few shifts. This? This is ridiculous, not to mention dangerous."

Suddenly, he slammed a fist on his desk. It cracked and the wood splintered down the middle. "See?" He growled.

I wasn't looking at a terrifying, out of control werewolf: I was looking at my scared Dad.

"I've been putting off addressing this for too long. It's time for me to see someone of importance about this. I've been putting some time and thought into this, and I've also decided who."

He waited a breath before revealing this mysterious person. "I'm going to the Oracle."

I waited a beat. Another beat. And then- "The Oracle? Are we talking about the same thing? THE Oracle. She's the one that tells of prophecy and foretells the future. How in the world is she going to help you with your little anger management issues?"

Alpha Dame blinked slowly. "It won't just be for me. I want a couple answers on other things too. While I'm away, I will place my Beta in charge. I'm assuming you're going to Alpha Phoenix's pack today?"

I nodded.

"Alright then. I will be leaving in a days time. Go out and tell them the news: I haven't the courage to face them yet."

I offered him a sympathetic smile and just as I turned to go, he called out," And Adira?"

I glanced at him and he looked like he was about to say something of importance, but then he seemed to change his mind. He sighed and instead said," Tell them I'm busy, and to please not enter my office while I'm working."

I nodded again and left without saying a word, because really, what else was there to say? I was glad he was finally getting that checked out. It wasn't normal for your wolf to be super dominant, especially an Alpha's. He should have had it in check by now, but since he didn't he was going to see the Oracle about it.

It was strange though. Of all he could see, The Oracle was who he chose? I would have thought the most famous of werewolf doctors, or even the Werewolf King's healer. We were, after all, one of the most well known and respected packs in the country.

I decided not to dwell too much on it, for I had my own problems I had to focus on. The main one stood not even 10 feet away from me. His violet eyes bore into mine, and I could feel him assessing me. Not for the first time, my mind went to the white wolf in the clearing. I knew it was impossible that this was him, because human wise they didn't even look the same.

And that's when my wolf, Rose, spoke up. It was dark, you might not have gotten a good look.

Please, my eyesight is amazing. I would know. I mentally scoffed, and imagined myself haughtily lifting my nose in the air like some pompous princess.

It's the same violet eyes, Ira.

Wouldn't he have recognized me, then?

Even if he did, doesn't mean he would tell you just yet. He keeps a lot of secrets from you.

I'll talk to you later- in private. I then blocked her and focused on the present.

"You okay?" I heard Phoenix ask, and I smiled to reassure him.

"Yes, I'm fine. I've actually got to talk to my family right now, so..."

"I'm staying by your side, majesty."

"Majesty?" I let a short breath of air escape in what could pass as a laugh if need be. "That's my nickname?"

He nodded, looking completely and utterly serious. "Yes. You're just as powerful and fierce, and wrenchingly beautiful like the royals."

Braxton cleared his throat. "So? Is he going to come out and apologize?"

"He's going to see someone about it. He's going to the Oracle." Immediately, he burst out in questions like I did, as did Xavier but with more reserved grace. My mother was oddly quiet and I decided to ask her about it later. Instead, I answered some of their questions. "Yes, I'm serious. No, not joshing. He needs to find out why his wolf is so strong, and how to fix it. He's in his office right now, though, and doesn't want to be bothered."

"By why the Oracle?" My brother persisted, his hands moving. "Why not a doctor?"

I sighed. "I don't know, Brax. I'm going to go pack up now. I.." I swallowed, the words suddenly hard to get out. "I have to go."

Both boys glanced at Alpha Phoenix, who stood there with an undecipherable look on his face. Either they both thought they would be able to speak to me later, after I packed up, or they were too afraid of my mate. Either way, they both chorused," Ok."

And left, walking out the front door. I knew them, and also knew they would be back when Phoenix wasn't around.

"Alpha Pho-"

"Phoenix." He interrupted, holding out a hand. "Just Phoenix."

"Okay, then. Phoenix. Give me an hour. Is that doable? And you can call and plan and catch up on your Alpha work."

"Yes, that's fine. I'll give you some space, and will be waiting for you outside this pack house."

"Sounds like a plan." I said, then waited for him to leave. When he didn't, I took it as the cue to head to my room.

As I walked away, I saw him take out his phone and hold it to his ear. He was speaking in serious tones, and I wondered if he was telling whoever was on the other end about us being mates. I could only hope I made the right choice by choosing to go back to his pack with him.

CHAPTER 6

I was packed and ready to go. I said good-bye to Trish, which consisted of lots of tears on her end, and sad reassurance on my end. After 40 minutes of this, I had to tear myself away by promising her," I'll call."

Then she would bomb me with more demands, and I would manage to slip in," Yes, I'll try to call everyday, no promises though."

She was satisfied with this, and let me go after 5 more minutes of tears.

My mom was waiting for me by the door, and she grabbed my shoulders and pulled me towards her and whispered in my ear, "Till our grave."

"Till our grave." I echoed. I thought it was strange she was making me promise again not to tell about my healing abilities, but I knew she was looking out for my well being. There were no tears involved, because we weren't the crying type.

Xavier and Brax were hard to say good-bye to, too. They weren't as emotional as Trish, but I could feel their reluctance as they gave me a hug and whispered words of encouragement. I made Brax promise to take care of the family and his mate, and tell me when he found out I became an Aunt.

I ordered Xavier to continue the training where I left off, but I knew he would have done it whether I asked him to or not. I knew he was sad and angry that I was leaving, but he also couldn't help but feel content that I had found myself a mate.

"But if he treats you like anything less than a Queen, you call me and I'm getting you out of there." Xavier vowed, holding my gaze.

"I will." I whispered, then drew him in for a fierce hug. I feared that if I let him go, I would never see him again. I always told myself I hated him for trying to get us a mate bond, but I knew he was just looking out for me, in his own way. Just like my mother.

"Let's go." Phoenix's voice cut through our parting, and I let go with a sad smile.

"I'll see you soon." I promised all three of them, then turned to leave and didn't look back.

It would have been harder that way, watching their sad faces begging me to come back, to stay, so I kept trudging forward with my head down. I knew my father would come to see me at Alpha Phoenix's pack and see how I was coping before going on his journey to find the Oracle, so I chose not to bother him in his office.

It was silent as we walked to where his car was situated, but I was used to that by now. I enjoyed it, and made it a point not to break it. The silence was welcomed and let me think without interruption.

That was, before he decided to break it. "We will first have to make a stop in Paris, for I have business to conduct before we go back to my pack in Yorkshire."

I stopped dead in my tracks. "Wait, what? You're kidding."

His face looked as serious as I've ever seen it. "No. Do I look like I'm kidding?"

"B-but that's all the way in England!" I exclaimed, my mouth hanging open. "We're in Nevada right now-"

"-I noticed-"

"And England is like millions of miles away!" My mind flashed back to when I promised my family and friends that I would visit them and I vowed not to break that promise. "I thought we were only an hour away, a few at the most. We are hopping countries here."

"I also noticed that." Phoenix's expression was cool, as was his voice. This was not okay.

"Look, do you have some of your pack stationed nearby or anything?" I asked, desperate.

He raised an eyebrow and shook his head. "No."

I groaned and covered my face with my hands. "Ugh. How am I going to keep my promise, then?"

"Your promise?" He questioned, now looking slightly curious.

I glowered. "Don't pretend you didn't hear. I made a vow to visit them often, and I intend to uphold it."

He made a tsking sound between his teeth. "Never make promises you can't keep." He said gravely, then muttered so low I almost thought I imagined it," Learned that from experience."

By now I could see the car. I considered making a run for it, but how far would I get? Not that far. Now that I knew from experience. Besides, I'm sure he would let me visit them every once in awhile if I asked. He himself said he acted like a conceited ass to get the reaction of me, that's not his 'real' personality. So I can only hope that he's super nice and sympathetic at heart, because I haven't seen the real him yet.

To be honest, that bothered me. When mates meet, they should be really happy, thrilled and excited to finally meet their mate. It's not every day you get to meet your soulmate: only once are you allowed that opportunity. But I wasn't thrilled or happy. I was scared. And I tried to escape TWICE. But for some reason, I found myself back in his sights and I don't mind. He just has to prove himself to me and we'll be great.

As I slipped inside the shotgun of the car, with Phoenix in the driver's seat, I flashbacked to a few minutes ago.

'Till our Grave.' My mother always talked about how I had to keep that secret. My ability was unnatural, and not how the daughter of an Alpha should be. I was a freak, and she wanted to keep it a secret at any and all tabs. That meant if me and Phoenix started the mate bond...then he would know.

He would know my secret.

I frowned at my discovery, and found myself tearing up. I felt a hand on my arm and I jumped in surprise. "You'll be able to visit." Phoenix said softly.

That wasn't the reason I was tearing up, but I nodded anyways and looked out the window. He took his hand away, and the warmth with it. I shivered, and I felt him glance at me.

"Are you alright? I have a jacket in the back." He offered, and I took a deep breath, getting ready for what I had to do. I had to push him away so he didn't like me. So he hated me, and eventually decided to reject me. That's the only way I would stay safe, and him as well. Because if my secret was discovered, who knew who would be after me and because he was my mate, also him?

I had to keep him safe, and this was the only way.

"I didn't ask for your help." I snapped, my tone harsh.

He let out a breath through his nose, but otherwise didn't comment.

I already felt awful, and felt my walls rise up around my heart. I wasn't sure how long I could keep this up for, but it was for our own good.

My wolf whined, and I could feel her itching to reach out to his wolf to explain my sudden mood change.

No, don't do it I commanded her, my patience thin and emotions scattered.

He's hurt, she argued, and whined again.

It's for his own good: you know why I have to do this

There was no answer after that.

I decided to do one of the things I was good at and sleep. I rested my head against the car door, ignoring the bumps and vibrations. Instantly I fell into a deep sleep, unaware of the eyes watching me.

Phoenix POV

"I didn't ask for your help." She snapped, but it seemed like she holding back more tears.

I refrained from snapping back, instead letting out a frustrated breath through my nose. This girl would be the death of me.

She was definitely hiding something from me about her, something important. I saw the way she looked at me: she was scared. Not of me, but for me. And I knew what she was playing at.

Trying to push me away so I would hate her and not care for her, so I would be safe? Please. I've tried that before and it didn't work. That's how I know what she was doing.

But what was her secret? The one she was so adamant to keep from me, the one where even her mother made her promise, "Till our grave."

Maybe that's not what her mother was even referencing to, but I'm pretty good at connecting the dots, and there are a LOT of dots.

Out of the corner of my eye, I saw her lean against the window and in no time was out cold. The only sign of her being alive was the steady rise and fall of her chest.

I took this time to mind link some of the members of my pack.

We should be arriving in the airport in an hour. From there it will take 8 hours on plane to get to Paris, and from there, after a few days when my business is done, 3 hours to Yorkshire. I will tell you when we are an hour away from the pack. I told my Beta, and he replied instantly.

Yes, Alpha. And in which room will she be staying?

For now, the guest room connected to mine. Don't get me wrong, I wanted her in my room as much as any other werewolf who just found their mate, but I knew I would have to take it slow with her. In no time, we were at the airport and I was gently shaking her shoulder, sparks igniting from where my hand and fingers made contact with her skin.

She stirred, a smile gracing her soft, pink lips. I took a second to study her and once again became fascinated with how beautiful she was. Her pale skin was blemish free, and framing it was her light blonde hair. She had a straight, somewhat button nose and a few freckles scattering the bridge of her nose.

"Stop it, Brax I'm up!" She half groaned, half yelled and I felt a pang in my heart.

"We're at the airport." I said, my hand still on her bare arm.

She looked at me with a little bit of confusion before realization dawned on her. It was truly amazing the change in her face and eyes: a shutter closed behind them and her bow lips pursed before realizing I was staring at her quite intently.

Adira blushed, her pale face turning a deep red. I smirked, and she tilted her head subtly so her hair covered half of her face. I don't think she realized she did that, but she did it when she got self-conscious.

"Sorry." She muttered, and waved it off.

"It's fine. We're at the airport, Adira. It's going to be a long trip on the plane to Paris, so anything you want at the airport tell me and I'll get it for you for the trip. After after a few days there, we will head to Yorkshire, which will only be a few hours by plane."

"Ok." She didn't look at me as she stepped out the car and grabbed her bags.

I decided to let her be and see how long she could keep it up. "Follow me."

CHAPTER 7

W ow. I'd read a lot about Paris, and seen lots of pictures, but nothing could have prepared me for what I saw. The minute we stepped out of the plane, I almost got run over by a large suitcase.

I let out a yelp and a hand pushed me out of harms way. Amused violet eyes looked down at me. "Careful, majesty, some of these French are ruthless."

A surprised laugh came out of my mouth and I slapped a hand over it. "Did you just almost-kind- of make a joke?" I looked at him, my eyes wide with shock.

He play frowned. "Don't look so shocked. I can be a funny guy if I want to."

I crossed my arms and raised an eyebrow. He mimicked me and I stared at him. "Who are you and what did you do with Phoenix-"

I paused, realizing I didn't even know his full name. "What's your last name?" I asked, my gaze searching his.

"Lansel."

"-Who are you and what have you done with Phoenix Lansel?" I demanded, my hands propped on my hips.

He laughed, shoulders shaking. "It's still me. The real Phoenix." He smiled, and I shook my head at him before realizing what I was doing. We were bantering like some old married couple, even though I had successfully managed to give him the cold shoulder for 4 hours, not that I was keeping track or anything.

I suddenly dropped my gaze from his and picked up my suitcase, my strength allowing me to do so with ease. "Where we headed now?"

Phoenix glanced at his watch and then took his phone out of his pocket. "Our driver should be here any minute."

While we waited, we walked over to a small cafe and set out luggage down by a small table. I sat in one of the chairs and watched as he ordered two caramel mochas with whipped cream and chocolate syrup.

I narrowed my eyes when I saw girls of various ages eyeing him up and down quite obviously. Even some mothers did it with their husbands right next to them. I don't know what came over me, but I just had to show everybody he was mine: all mine, nobody else's.

I put my luggage on our chairs to save our spot and walked up to Phoenix from behind, wrapping my arms around his waist. He was still talking to the guy receiving orders, but he took my arms away from his waist and instead moved me so I was in front of him, his arms looped around my shoulders and hands folded in front of my stomach.

The cashier nodded as soon as Phoenix stopped talking, signaling he got the order.

As if Phoenix knew why I was there, he placed a swift kiss on my temple and moved with me to our seats. I pulled away from him as soon as he moved his suitcase from off his seat, but he grabbed me from my waist and sat me on his lap. "Where do you think you're going?" He murmured in my ear, and I looked around uncomfortably.

"Um, back to my seat?" I whispered back, conscious of the eyes on us.

"Why are you so self conscious about sharing a seat? Just a minute ago you went up to me and gave me a hug from behind, and even let me kiss you on the side of the head."

He had a point, but I simply shrugged. "Those girls were looking at you."

"Which girls?" Phoenix asked, voice low.

I frowned. "All of them."

He burst out laughing and I jumped, startled. Everyone looked away and I found myself smiling despite myself. As I looked at him, I knew then my first impression of him was wrong. Rumors were the worst, especially when all they did was destroy the reputation of the one the rumors were about. But that meant I had to try even harder to stay away and build a wall between us. If he was super nice and sweet, I couldn't risk him being hurt because of me. I would never forgive myself.

The minute our coffee's were called, I hopped off his lap and grabbed mine, looking anywhere but him when he grabbed his and went to stand next to me. "Is our driver here yet?" I asked impatiently, still surveying the crowds.

Phoenix was silent. I looked up at him and he had an expression on his face I couldn't decipher. As soon as he looked down at me, I turned my face away. A minute passed by with us awkwardly sipping our coffee's and not looking at each other. Well, I don't know about him, but that's what I was doing.

At long last, our 'driver' came up to us. He had slicked back blond hair and sunglasses on, and he held his arms out in front of me. After a beat I realized he wanted to take the bags, but I shook my head.

"Miss, please let me take your bags." His voice was deep and scratchy, like he didn't use it often.

Still, I stubbornly refused. "I've got it." I insisted.

Phoenix whispered something in the man's ear so low I couldn't hear, and then the driver nodded once and started walking away.

When I didn't move, confused, Phoenix raised an eyebrow and swept an arm outward. "After you, tigress." He didn't smile or smirk after he said the nickname. Guilt swirled in my stomach from the way I was treating him.

All I did was offer a tight smile and catch up to the driver. It was only a minute walk to our car, which turned out to be a limousine. "Wow." My eyes widened and Phoenix opened the back door for me.

"Get in."

I obeyed, not saying a word. I surveyed the inside and found a fully stocked mini fridge with soda and beer. The seats were black and very soft, and they faced both ways. Phoenix sprawled out on the seats across from me and said," Get some sleep, it'll be a few hours before we make it to the hotel."

I didn't want to argue and I was feeling pretty tired, so I stretched out and closed my eyes. Only a few seconds passed before I fell into darkness.

"We're here." I awoke to Phoenix shaking my arm and got a moment of deja vu.

I tried to see outside the windows, but they were tinted. The door opened and bright light seeped in. I blinked and clambered outside on unsteady legs. I was still waking up, and was disoriented. Where were we?

We stood in front of a huge mansion, and a sign that looked to be decorated with gold hung on one of the top floors. It read," Hotel Bachelor." The bright lights were coming from the open the door that some random guy was holding open for us. It was dark outside: I guess night had fallen while I was asleep.

"We're staying here?" I asked Phoenix, and he nodded, walking past me. I followed.

The second we got inside, I thought there had to be some sort of mistake. Chandeliers hung around the high ceilings, and decorative trim surrounded the huge room. We seemed to be in the lobby, and another grand room was connected to it. It was a ball room, or some kind of dancing hall because music was playing and their were couples dancing. The girls had on beautiful dresses, and the men were in tux's. They all had masks on.

"This must cost like a million dollars!" I hissed at Phoenix, embarrassed we had walked into the wrong hotel.

He gazed at me coolly and walked up to the registration desk as if he hadn't even heard me. I watched dumbfounded as he gracefully made his way back to where I stood with a key in his hand. "Thank you, Andrew."

The driver nodded and left, leaving just me and my mate.

"Erm, you only have one key..."

I fidgeted under his intense stare. "I know." Was his reply.

"But I thought we were getting separate rooms?" I said it as a question, and he smirked.

"You thought wrong. Now follow me and try to keep up." He abruptly strode away from me at a fast pace.

I chased after him, passing many people and all of them were dressed up. I looked down at my jeans and t-shirt and cringed. "Adira!" I heard Phoenix yell, and I hurried to catch up.

"Right here."

After walking down a few hallways and turning about 4 times, we made it to our room: 32. He put the key in and turned it, then pushed it open.

The room was very large, with white carpet and a large balcony where we could look out over the city. I saw the Eiffel tower and grinned wide, running inside. The bed was huge, and I jumped on it. It was the perfect mix of bouncy, soft, and firm. I instantly fell in love.

Phoenix took one look at me and chuckled. He set his stuff on one of the chairs by the door and grabbed boxers and shorts out of his bag. "I'm taking my shower real quick. See what's in the fridge and pantry."

As he closed the bathroom door behind him, I shot up from the bed. Food?! Where?

I saw another door that wasn't the one to the hallway or to the bathroom and I pranced over and swung it open. It was a whole other room! A bar was on the far side, and closer to where I was standing was a see-through freezer and refrigerator, as well as candy, chips, and just junk food in general. I squealed and ran to gather an armful.

I went back to the bed and dumped all the candy and chips I had grabbed in there just as Phoenix came out, wearing only a towel.

The atmosphere in the room suddenly became thick with something I wasn't ready to acknowledge. Water dripped from his wet hair and trailed down his chest, down past his abs and under the towel. I cleared my throat and he crossed his arms, muscles flexing.

Hot damn.

"Why...Uh, why aren't you dressed? Didn't you bring your clothes into the bathroom with you?" I mentally smacked myself for asking such a question but I couldn't go back now.

He tilted his head towards the bathroom. "I forgot my soap and shampoo."

"Orange and Vanilla." I said without thinking, and immediately threw a hand over my mouth.

He didn't say anything and went over to his bag, took out two bottles, and then showed them to me. "Orange spice is what I wash with, my cologne is Vanilla."

"It's a good combination." I commented, and realized I wasn't keeping him at a safe distance. It was way too easy to forget everything when I was around him, and I wasn't sure if that was a good thing or a bad thing. Unaware of my internal struggle, he stepped close to me. Without warning, he leaned in close and sniffed me. I felt his lips brush the hollow of my neck and couldn't hold back my shiver. I felt him smirk against my skin.

"Roses and lemon balm." Phoenix brushed a lock of hair away from my shoulder and I stepped back.

"You should take your shower." My voice was indifferent.

He gave me a knowing smile and disappeared into the bathroom, leaving me to wonder what exactly just happened.

I was dressed in my pj's, which consisted of a tank top and shorts and was laying in bed when he came out of the shower. His hair was dry and he had on shorts but no shirt. I averted my eyes and instead focused on making a pillow barrier with the tons of pillows that littered the room.

I felt the bed dip as he sat down on the other side but I focused solely on my task until I was done. "This is a pillow barrier. Meaning, you don't breach this side of the pillows." I instructed, my voice firm.

"What if I don't want anything between us?" Phoenix said in a husky voice, and I risked a glance.

Bad choice.

His eyes were dark and his gaze was on my lips, to my chest, then back to my lips. "Eyes up here, buddy." I snapped the third time his eyes went down to my chest.

All he did was turn off the lights. When it was dark, he whispered," Can't I admire what is mine?"

I had no answer, and turned on my side.

He sighed.

Despite taking two naps today, I was out cold the minute my head hit my pillow. I could only hope that in the morning, the pillow barrier was still there.

CHAPTER 8

S unlight streamed through a window, urging me to open my eyes. I yawned and turned my head into my pillow, blocking out some of the light. Just like I typically did every morning, I went to roll over and stretch.

That's when the problem's started. I suddenly became aware of the warmth running up and down my back and ass, and my legs were tangled up in somebody else's. My eyes shot open in alarm and I tried to disentangle myself but I heard a grunt and was pulled back into the same spooning position I was trying to escape.

"Phoenix." I whispered, trying to lift his arms.

No response. What the hell happened to the pillow barrier?!

"Go back to bed." He answered back, his voice all but a husky breath.

I clamped down the feelings that were rising in me and became adamant. I didn't want to be in this position with a guy I was supposed to keep my distance with: that was the reason for the pillows! But a fat lot of good that did me. Look where I am now.

I tried again, squirming to get out of his hold. "Phoenix!" I whisper-yelled at the exact same time his hands squeezed my hip. "Adira." He warned.

I yelped and jerked away, unable to hold stop myself. I took him by surprise and he exclaimed," Jeez, woman, what's got you so jumpy?"

There was a beat of silence. And then, he poked my side. I squealed and tried to get out of his hold but he pulled me back and trapped me between his arms. We were now in the position where he was on top of and I underneath. "So you're ticklish."

He said it as a statement, not a question, so I didn't answer him.

Phoenix grinned evilly and then tickled both of my sides with vigor. I shrieked and tried to punch him but he dodged every try, and so I tried to kick him. I managed a solid one on his stomach that probably hurt my foot more than it did him, but it did the job. He stopped for a second and that was all I needed.

I rolled over and off the bed, then sprung right up and eyed him warily. He was sprawled out on the bed with a lazy grin on his face. How did he manage to look so good right in the morning, when I probably looked like a dirty sock after it had been run over by 100 trucks and then dragged through mud?

Phoenix slowly sat up and stretched, light illuminating his perfect body. I spotted a small mandala on his right hip and couldn't help but wonder what the stories were behind each tattoo.

"Like what you see?" Phoenix asked, the smirk never leaving his face.

Instead of getting flustered, I popped out my hip and placed a hand on it, ever so subtly arching my back. "Maybe. Do you like what you see?"

His answer was to pin me to the door. "Yes." He whispered right above my lips.

I swallowed and turned away, ruining the moment. "Liar. I probably look god awful like I always do in the morning. I'm going to take my shower."

Undeterred, he grabbed a lock of my hair. "You don't look god awful. And you don't have to take a shower- you smell amazing and you look gorgeous. Besides,"-

He stepped back, finally allowing me to breath,"-we don't have time. We overslept. We have to be on the road in 10 minutes, so pack your bags. When you're done, meet me outside. I'll be waiting for you."

Phoenix grabbed his suitcase and was about to walk out the door without a shirt on. Rolling my eyes, I picked up his forgotten shirt from the ground. I ran over to him and touched his bare back.

"You forgot your shirt, doofus." I said, handing it to him.

He grinned and snatched the shirt from my grasp. "Who said I forgot it?"

I stared at him. And stared. Finally, he laughed. "Just kidding, majesty. I wanted to see what you would do."

I raised an eyebrow and shoved him out the door after he pulled it over his head. Phoenix turned to me before he closed the door and tapped an imaginary wrist watch. "10 minutes."

10 minutes later and we were driving away from the fancy hotel. I was somewhat sad we wouldn't be staying there longer, but I took some of the food with me when we left.

When I mentioned it to Phoenix, he didn't seem surprised. "I know."

My brow furrowed. "How do you know? You weren't even in the room with me!"

He looked over at me with eyes that said are you dumb. "I can smell it."

My cheeks burned and I crossed my arms. "In my defense, I love food."

"I can tell." He said, and when he realized what he said he rushed to make amends. "I didn't mean you're fat or anything. You're not, you're skinny and perfect I really didn't mean-"

"It's fine." I held a hand up and chuckled, and soon he joined in the laughing.

A loud ringing noise filled the car we were in and I jumped, my eyes drawn to the console. Rose was the name, and right next to it was a phone.

"Who is that?" I asked, instantly suspicious.

"It's nobody, just ignore it." Phoenix said, but a smile danced on his lips.

I did the exact opposite of what he told me to do. "Answer."

The car heard my command and the call was turned on, allowing Rose to speak to Phoenix. "Hey honey."

She started out, and right away my opinion of her was below 0. "Where are you? Those Rogue prisoners you captured a couple of weeks ago are getting out of hand and I just don't know how much longer we an hold them off!"

"Rosey, listen to me-" Phoenix started, but she cut him off as if she didn't hear him.

"-I want you home as soon as possible because I've missed you so much!"

Ok, that's it.

"Um, who the hell are you and why are you calling my mate "Honey." He is mine and not yours, so back off." I fired out, too caught up in my temper to realize 'Rose' might be a human or a relative of his. The fact that I had little self control was looked down upon, and I was suddenly afraid to look at Phoenix.

He did the last thing I expected. His face lit up and he turned to me and whispered the words," Thank you," to me. Phoenix then faced the front again and said at a much louder volume,"Rose, I would like you to unofficially meet my mate, Adira. Adira, I would like you to meet my older sister, Rosey."

"It's a pleasure to meet you." Rose said on the other end of the line, and the tone of her voice suggested she was highly amused.

"Um, you too." I choked out after a stretch of awkward silence.

"Right. Okay, what do you want?" My mate asked his sister, and she answered without pausing.

"Can't I just call my baby brother to see how he is?"

Phoenix scowled when she called him her baby brother and I smirked. My arms had uncrossed and I reached inside my bag and pulled out a bag of chips. Opening them, I peered inside only to be greatly disappointed. There were literally only 5 chips. I took them out one by one and slowly ate them.

crunch. crunch. crunch. crunch-

"Adira, could you be any louder?" Phoenix sighed. I kept chomping away.

"Silence, peasant." I retorted, and after finishing my last chip I rummaged through my bag for another one. Finding a new bag of Classic Lays chips, I grinned with victory and opened it up and continued to eat.

Phoenix addressed Rose after a mock glare my way. "Any-ways, what did you really want? Because if it's nothing, then hang up. I've got other's I need to call."

Rose answered swiftly," It's about the Rogue's. More specif-ically, The Rogue."

The instant she mentioned 'The Rogue', Phoenix's grip on the steering wheel went knuckle-whitening tight and he grit his teeth. With his jaw locked, it was hard for him to speak but when he finally did, it was strained. "What about it."

"He...um, escaped." Rose said it with the most hesitant voice I've ever heard.

Without warning, Phoenix slammed his fist in the steering wheel, causing it to BEEEP long and loud. He cursed almost as loud as the car honking, and I was all of a sudden very scared to be in the same car with him.

"And..Um, killed a f-few on his way out." Rose continued, and I shook my head in a hopeless attempt to get her to stop talking. I knew she couldn't see me, but I tried nevertheless.

"How much is a few." He asked, his voice deadly calm. I crossed my fingers. Don't answer, please for the love of everything alive don't answer-

"23."

Phoenix glared at the road with murderous intent, and I slunk down in my seat so I had less of a chance to catch his attention. I don't want to die today. I plan to have a full, long life filled with unicorns and rainbows and fluffy kittens.

Emphasis on the fluffy kittens. And chicken nuggets, of course. Can't forget the chicken nuggets.

"I'm on my way to a meeting. It should take all but an hour. After that, me and Adira will catch another flight to Yorkshire England and we will meet you at the Pack House. Expect our arrival in 5 hours. Have the Beta and Delta there, along with the top 4 pack warriors and our parents. Also, the dungeon keeper will need to have a talking to. I'll do that on my own terms."

I shivered involuntarily by the way he said the last two sentences. I will not want to be there when the Dungeon Keeper has a talking to by Alpha Phoenix.

"Alpha Phoenix-" I quietly verbalized, and he turned to me with angry eyes.

"How many time do I have to goddamn tell you, it's Phoenix to you, not Alpha!" His voice rose to a loud shout until by the end of the sentence he was practically screaming at me.

I leaned away from him, but then I remembered that this was the way my Dad had used to act. In his fits, I had to stay strong and not back down. My body language changed and I sat up straight. My gaze was piercing and I met his stormy violet eyes.

"You are an Alpha, Alpha Phoenix. And I will address you as such. Calm down and think about what you're saying, how you're saying it, and to whom." My voice was gentle but stern. I sent a silent prayer up to the Moon Goddess that this worked.

His shoulders lowered from their original tense state, and his grip on the wheel loosened considerably. His head bowed in..what was that? Shame? It couldn't be.

His eyes remained trained on the road however, and then he glanced over at me with regret playing over his symmetrical features. "I'm sorry, love. My temper got the best of me. I'm just.." He let out a breath through his nose and finished. "..just scared."

My brow furrowed in disbelief and slight awe. Was an Alpha really telling me how he felt? Alpha's were known to keep a close reign on their emotions. I didn't want to let this moment slip from my grasp, so I asked," Who is the Rouge Wolf? Is he anyone I would know?"

Phoenix's countenance went from bleak to harsh. "I hope you don't know him, majesty. I hope to the Moon Goddess you don't."

Chapter 8 is done! Whoo:3

Please tap the star and vote if you liked the moments between Phadira in this chapter! It really is important to me and encourages me to keep on writing:)

Also, if anyone wants to make other covers for me of this book, I will pick some of the best ones and dedicate a chapter to you and will use my favorite cover, as well as the one the readers comment on the most.

Love you my pandas,

~White-Rabbit

2,078 words

CHAPTER 9

"You may sit." The man at the head of the table looked to be in his late 50's at least, but it was clear he held a lot of power. His black hair was peppered with grey around the edges, and his dark eyes held little emotion. I fought the urge to cower when his empty eyes landed on me.

Phoenix and the other 7 sat down, and I followed suit. Phoenix made sure I was sitting next to him, and for that I was grateful. I knew it was his possessive side coming out, even though I don't know why it would come out now. Most of the guys at the table were old enough to be my grandpa.

Yeah, not exactly my type.

"You all are here for a specific reason. I called you here to talk about the rising problem of the Rogue's. They are starting to attack the weaker packs and holding them as prisoner. This is getting out of hand, so I've gathered us together to think of a solution."

"The Rogue's have a king." I stated simply after he was done speaking. All eyes turned to me in surprise, and I didn't even get to finish what I was about to say before the man verbally attacked me.

" Sorry, men. It seems we have someone in our midst that I didn't expect to see or hear. Frankly, I don't even know why the pup is here." His voice was cold, and a few chuckles escaped those around the table. I narrowed my eyes and just managed to hold myself back from snarling at him. Just as I was about to defend myself, Phoenix put a hand on my knee under the table and mind linked, let me take care of this.

I watched him with a poker face, making sure no one knew what I was thinking. I wanted to teach this man a lesson. Who did he think he was, calling me a pup? That was extremely offensive. I guess I wasn't very good at hiding my emotions, because he smirked when he saw my reaction.

"Why did she even bother talking? Why did she think we were going to put up with her worthless-"

"Are you done attacking my mate, Adam?" Phoenix said harshly, though his face was calm.

Adam's face didn't change. "Oh, so she's your mate. And that makes it all right for her to be here? If I wasn't in such a good mood today, she would be out of her faster than you can say Rogue."

"I would like to see you try to take her away from me." His hand found mine under the table and squeezed, and I squeezed back.

Adam looked at me once again, dismissing Phoenix. My mouth flattened in a straight line. He thought he had the power to dismiss Alpha Phoenix of the Blood Ash Pack? Well, he apparently did because all my mate did was clench his teeth. Phoenix didn't say anything, which was not his usual reaction when someone disrespected him.

At this point, I was not conscious of my actions. I stood up so fast my chair shot behind me and slammed into the wall, making a loud booming noise resonate throughout the room. "Don't you dare disrespect Alpha Phoenix of the Blood Ash pack, old man, and don't you dare disrespect me. I am not a pup, I am to be a Luna soon, and you should not forget that!"

My voice rang with authority and was so powerful, even I was shocked at how cogent it sounded. Dead silence was met with my declaration and I retrieved my chair and sat down gracefully. Folding my hands, aware of all the eyes on me, I tilted my head in Adam's direction. "Now, may I continue?"

Instead of answering my question directly, Adam's mouth tilted up in a twisted smile. "I underestimated you. I don't plan to do that ever again. What is your name?"

"Adira Sabrina Dame, previously known as the daughter of the Alpha of the Moonhigh pack, but soon to be Luna of the Blood Ash pack."

He nodded once. "A rank I will not forget."

Adam then folded his hands in front of him on the table and said," Continue. I'm curious to what you will suggest."

I took a deep breath. "Why not attack them where it will hurt them the most? We could capture the Rogue King. Without their leader, they'll be like lost puppies trying to find their way home."

"Capture the Rogue King? Do you know what you're suggesting?" One of the men sitting diagonal from me spoke up, his head already glistening from sweat.

"Yes." I said slowly, speaking as if he was slow. "I know exactly what I am suggesting."

Their bewildered looks were enough to make me want to laugh, but I refrained, instead keeping my features as cool and neutral as possible.

"And I think with the right planning, timing, and people, we could pull it off."

"Then please, by all means, indulge me. What exactly is the plan?" Adam asked, leaning back in his imposing swivel chair.

Oh geez. That's the part I haven't quite figured out yet. But of course I couldn't let that slip. I had to fake it till I make it, and so that's exactly what I did. I remembered the Royal Ball was getting held soon, and decided to use that in my plan.

"The King and Queen will be at the huge ball being held in two months. The Royal Ball. And it will be our job to get invited to it."

"Who is we?" Adam asked, and I looked around the room. "Me and Phoenix, obviously. I'm not sure what station and rank the rest of you are, so if this plan is to your liking, we will work out the details later."

Once he nodded, I took it as my cue to continue. "We invite the Rogue King as some sort of false security, maybe say we want to make amends and have a peace treaty. And then we kidnap him on the way to the Ball or at the Ball, whatever will look less suspicious and apparent."

Phoenix pointed out in a composed voice,"I know some of The Royal's personally. If we wanted this to take place, I could get it to happen. I would be able to get us invitations, but I'm not sure about the rest of you. Adam, since you're one of their personal advisors, what do you think about this plan?"

My eyes almost bugged out of my head and I regarded Adam with more respect. Instantaneously, I recalled the way I spoke to him and cringed.

Nobody seemed aware of my internal struggle. Adam studied his folded hands before coming to a decision. "We might be able to pull it off. With the right planning and precise timing, this Rogue problem could come to an end in no time."

He shifted his eyes to look at me and he smiled. It still didn't hold any real warmth to it, but it did hold some respect. I lifted my chin in confidence. I would take what he gave me.

"Good work, Adira. You all may go. I will call you back if need be, so always be on alert. I have some pressing matters to attend to at the Palace. And Alpha Phoenix?"

When his eyes were on him, Adam said,"You and your mate especially should be ready. The Royal Ball is, as Adira said, only two months away. For this to work will need lots of planning and scheming, all before that time. You two will be a big part of this, in ways I don't think you can imagine."

With that, he got up from his chair and exited the room, leaving us.

"What was that?" Phoenix demanded the second we got in the car.

"What was what?"

He didn't turn the car on just yet. Instead, he turned in his seat to face me. "You just called the personal advisor of the King and Queen of our werewolf community an old man. Do you know what would have happened if he felt disrespected? He could have ruined my name!"

Getting fed up, I countered," I defended myself! He verbally attacked me and I didn't like what he was saying."

"Jesus, Adira, I told you I would deal with it!"

I snapped. "But you didn't!"

The silence was heavy, weighing down on my shoulders but I pressed on. "You said you would deal with it but you didn't. You didn't stand up for me when he called me a pup and mocked me, you just shut up when he dismissed you. Instead, I was the one that did and you're not even proud of me. And shit, Phoenix, that's all you care about? Your damn reputation?"

I shook my head, beyond words. "Just drive."

Phoenix was quiet. When he didn't make any move to pull out of the parking space, I whirled around to face him, only to find our faces inches apart. I froze, not breathing. His violet eyes were bright, and filled with something I didn't recognize. "He is powerful, majesty. I don't think you realize that. He might even be more powerful than the King and Queen themselves, since he basically tells them what to do. But do you know what he is most known for?"

He seemed to be waiting for an answer, so I bit my lip and quietly said," No."

He abided. "His temper is horrible. It's like a raging, living beast. And if he gets triggered, he will quite literally destroy anything in a couple yard radius. Nobody talks back to him because they know what will happen if they do. I'm sorry for not warning you earlier. And I'm sorry for snapping at you."

Phoenix leaned back, running a hand over his face. "I just don't want to see you hurt. You worry me with that temper, majesty. It's going to get you in real trouble some day and I won't be there to protect you."

Unexpectedly, loud bangs were heard right near where we were. The next few seconds happened in a blur. Shots ricochet off the car and Phoenix dove at me, his body pressing mine down. "Get down! Lower the seat so it's flat and crawl in the backseat: I'm covering you."

"Hurry!" He yelled when I didn't move.

I scrambled to the back of the car and managed not to get hit. Glass shattered, raining down on me. I dragged my body through the glass and rested under the seats so I was protected.

The car door opened and I let out a strangled," Phoenix, no!" When I saw him walk towards the shooters from my tilted view of the outside world. He paid no attention to me and kept walking confidently, hands out.

There were two men dressed in all black complete with a mask with two guns, and they were hiding behind a wall. As Phoenix was about to reach them, they started firing shots wildly. Knowing I couldn't just lay there and let him die, I rolled out of my spot, opened the car door quietly and landed stealthily on my feet.

Just as I was about to speed over there, a cool blade pressed against my neck and I was drawn against a firm body. "Easy there, Princess. Stay silent and it'll all be over soon."

The voice was deep sounding and a male's, but it didn't sound old. The arms trapping me against him was strong, and I could feel his muscles through his shirt. I would have to act fast if I wanted to get out this alive.

I let out a yell and head butted backward. My captor cursed and his hold on me loosened enough that I could grab his arms around my neck with the knife in his hand and yank him forward. He stumbled forward a couple of feet and I was able to get a good look at him.

He was gorgeous, with messy blond hair and emerald green eyes. He was dressed in all black but his face wasn't covered, which was how I could see his perfect look. I had to keep in mind he was my enemy, though, which was hard to do when he stood there, smiling with dimples on each cheek.

"Look, I don't want to hurt you–"

I rushed forward, intending to knock him out but all he did was sigh as if I was a nuisance. Moving faster than I could see him, we were back in the same position as before, except this time the knife was digging into my neck. I feared if I even took a deep breath, it would cut the skin. I tried to steady my breathing, but when I saw Phoenix effortlessly killing the two guards, a gasp escaped me. The knife scraped across my skin and I felt a slight stinging and warm blood trickle down my neck.

"Stay still." The young man hissed in my ear, his hold on me tightening. Was that regret I heard in his voice?

No, it couldn't be because the moment Phoenix turned around and spotted us, my captor yelled," Stay where you are or she bleeds more!"

Phoenix froze, and I lifted my chin and gave him a grim smile. I mind linked him It's going to be okay, Phoenix. Stay strong for me.

"No!" He yelled, his face contorted in agony. He realized I was accepting my fate. The fact that I mind linked him told him that as well. Mind linking required a great deal of strength, and I just used some of mine to tell him to be strong for me.

Blond backed up, taking me with him and approached a car I hadn't even noticed. Too late now, I thought to myself sadly. "Adira!" Phoenix shouted, taking a step in my direction. Blond stopped and pressed me closer to him, and I closed my eyes tight.

"I told you to stay put." His voice was hard, and when I opened my eyes again, Phoenix looked at me with a look I will never forget. Love, Anger, and determination.

"I will find you, majesty." He vowed.

That was the last thing I heard before someone hit the back of my head and I fell into darkness.

CHAPTER 10

I woke up in stages.

The first stage was pain. There was a pounding in my head that wouldn't stop, and the pain was starting from the back of my head. My neck throbbed, and my whole body was sore.

The second stage were the sounds. There were slams and banging noises that echoed within my skull. I winced, and that led me to the third stage.

Awareness. I pried open my eyes slowly, afraid of what I would see. Bright white walls filled my vision with vigor, half blinding me. I groaned and shut them right away again. And then I heard the voices right by my bedside, which I realized had been there for a while but only now was I making sense of the sounds.

"...couldn't help it. I had to knock her out!"

"No you didn't. Well, you had to knock her out-"

"-Exactly!-"

"-But not by hitting her in the back of the head! You could have covered her mouth and nose with the rag. It was already drenched in sleeping potion, ready for you in the plastic bag in the dashboard. Now I'm not sure what her injuries are. They are probably so much worse now, because of you!" The second, high-pitched voice rose to a shout and I let out a sound.

Immediately the voices quieted and I felt a cold and clammy hand on my forehead. "Open your eyes slowly, Adira."

I did as the person said without question. Blink, Blink, Blink. 5 blinks later and the room was in focus. I was in a white room, with two doors. I was laying in a bed with white covers, blankets and pillows. There was no color at all.

"How are you feeling?" The same voice asked, and I tried to find where it came from.

"Like shit." I responded, finally finding the source of the talking. Two people my age stood right beside me. One of them I recognized immediately. The one who kidnapped me. The other was a pretty girl, with black hair and crystal blue eyes. My sight was only set on one of them in particular, however.

I growled in anger and lunged at my kidnapper, but he sped away to the other side of the room. When I let out a yell and tried to get to him, arms encircled my waist and pinned me to the wall. "Calm down, we're not going to hurt you!"

The girl was digging her knee into my back and my headache slammed behind my eyes, but I was a werewolf and by god would not go down easily. I strained against her, yelling," Get off of me! Get the fuck off of me!"

This went on for a few more seconds before she grabbed the back of my neck and dropped the nice act. "Calm down. If you don't, we'll be forced to knock you out again. So shut up and sit down on the bed and everything will be explained to you."

I quickly thought it over in my head and knew that listening to her for now would be the best course of action. I would play nice until I found an opportunity to take them out and run. It would be smart to find out what they wanted and why they took me, though, so I clamped my mouth shut and stopped struggling.

The girl took her knee away from my back and stepped away from me cautiously. I glared at her but made my way to the bed and sat on it. The boy quirked an eyebrow at me and I folded my arms, but made sure to stay loose. I needed to be ready for anything.

They came around and stood at the foot of the bed. The bed itself wasn't very big, so they were closer to me than was comfortable. The girl spoke up first. "My name's Naomi, and this is-"

"-Alexander, at your service." The boy finished, winking.

I stared at him. "You just kidnapped me and you're winking at me?"

Naomi tried to suppress a smile, but from the way she was covering her mouth with her hand, she was failing. By the time she got serious, I knew there were three windows total in the room, and one of them wasn't locked and didn't have a screen. We looked to be in the second or third floor, and

I'm betting it's the third. The floor was hardwood, and there was nothing in here I could use as a weapon.

I'm not sure if Alexander noticed me checking out the room, but he was the one to warn me. "Don't try escaping. We have ways to make you stay here that you would not be happy with. Oh, the perimeters are always rigged just for you, so don't try getting of the property either. Just a friendly reminder." He smiled, all white teeth and dimples, and I scowled.

"Why did you kidnap me?" I asked, looking at both of them.

"Don't think of it as kidnapping. Think of it as..." Alexander struggled to find a word to replace kidnap, and when he did he smiled proudly. "A borrowing of you for a certain time period."

"Answer the question." I demanded, not letting him off the hook just because of his charms and looks.

Naomi decided that Alexander had messed around enough and answered the question bluntly. "We know what you are. You are known as The Caladrius, or the Pure Dove. There was someone else a thousand years ago named Lilia in the myth of Rhaknorisk. The Moon Goddess gave her these special powers, or abilities, to-"

I held up my hands. "Woah, let's slow down for a second and think about what you're saying. First off, what are you jabbering about with the whole me being a Dove? I'm not a bird, last time I checked."

She rolled her eyes. "Don't pull that crap, you know exactly what you are."

I let my face adopt the look of confusion. "What the heck are you talking about?"

Alexander studied me with a serious look on his face, and I struggled to keep the facade. No one was supposed to know about my ability, so how in the world did they? And they had a name for me, too? I remembered what I heard as I was waking up. 'Open your eyes slowly, Adira.' Naomi knew my name.

Could I trust them? No. They took me against my will and were trying to kill my mate. Or if not kill, at least seriously injure, because those shooters didn't look like they were going easy on the bullets. But they said they wouldn't hurt me, that Alexander wasn't supposed to knock me out by force, just a sleeping drug. I decided to tell them the truth but twist it a little bit.

"I don't know what you're yapping about with the whole 'Caladrius' thing. And for the whole me having a power, I think I would know if I had one."

Alexander stared at me hard. His face was all scrunched up, and suddenly he said," You're lying."

I picked one of my fingernails. It was a nervous habit that I couldn't control even if I tried. "What?"

I seemed to be saying that a lot lately.

"I'm a hybrid. Both werewolf and Fae, and can sense lies."

I stopped playing with my fingers and gaped at him. "Fae? Their extinct!"

He spread his arms wide and smirked. "Obviously not because here I am."

Perplexed, I bit the inside of my cheek before saying," But isn't it the other way around? The fae are the ones who can't do the lying, it's not that they can sense lies."

He nodded. "Well, that is also true. We can't tell any lies. But since I only have barely more than a quarter of fae blood in me, I can twist the truth and sense lies. The whole sensing lies part I think is just a bonus."

"Not for us." Naomi muttered, and Alexander laughed. It was a deep contagious laugh, and I chuckled before coming to terms with what I was doing. What was wrong with me? I kept forgetting that Alexander was the enemy, that Naomi was the enemy. I've got to get in the right mindset, for this back-and-forth, cat-and-mouse thing we've been doing has gone on long enough.

"Back to what I was saying." Naomi cut in, apparently thinking along the same lines as me. "You have powers. Healing powers, to be exact. And they have had to reveal themselves at one point, right?" She said, turning to Alexander for confirmation.

He pressed his lips together so they formed a thin line and gave his consent with a tilt of his head. She turned back to me. "So there you go. Have you ever healed anybody before? And please remember, we're not the enemy. I-"

She took a deep breath. "I'll make an oath on the Moon Goddess. I, Naomi Beverlies, swear on the Moon Goddess that all I'm trying to do is help you and will never purposefully hurt you."

My mouth dropped open. She just made an oath to the Moon Goddess, and which means if she backs out of her oath, she will die. I knew I could trust her, and when I cast a glance at Alexander, she hurriedly said,"You can trust him."

So I told them what happened that night, despite the promise to my mother. When I finished, they both looked at me in awe. "I knew it." Naomi whispered, and then she turned to Alexander.

"It's the Lost Hybrid."

I wanted to ask what that meant but Alexander repeated what she said before I could ask. "The Lost Hybrid, indeed. I will spread the word."

He left, and Naomi looked upon me and smiled kindly. "I really am sorry for the extreme measures we went to get you. Alexander was a little.."

Her eyes zeroed in on my neck and she frowned. "..rough. Let's patch you up, shall we?"

She opened the door and swept an arm for me to go before her. "Hybrid's first."

CHAPTER 11

I was once again sitting around a large table, except the person at the head of it was not an imposing man. Instead, there stood a lenient looking woman, with soft brown eyes and short, dirty blonde hair. Glasses were perched on top of her head, and her fingernails were done a pale rose pink.

Sitting around the table were others my age and a few years older, but none were younger. I knew this because they all introduced themselves to me at the beginning of this meeting with their name and 'station', which was a really fancy way of saying age.

The woman in the front cleared her throat and the room immediately became quiet. When she spoke, her voice was soft but rang clear. "You are all here today because of your special talents. We have gathered you from all over for many reasons, and a number of them were to find the Lost Hybrid. And she is here with us today, sitting at this table with us, whom all of you were introduced to."

My eyes widened. The Lost Hybrid? This was the first I was hearing about this. When everyone looked my way was an even greater surprise. I was the Lost Hybrid? All they told me before I was ushered out here was everything would be explained to me. I guess they wanted to tell me in front of an audience in case I decided to try anything.

"Adira, we promised to explain everything to you, and we will. And the best way we can tell you is by storytelling. But first, a little history on us and how we came to be, and some history on you."

Her voice soothed me, and I sat back to listen with a faint smile.

"Once upon a time, there was a great Queen. She was beautiful, kind, and gentle. However, she was not very smart. One day, as she was out in her castle gardens picking roses, a great White Wolf appeared to her."

Immediately I perked up. The White Wolf?

"The wolf was gorgeous, and the most outstanding feature of it,-" Here she paused, looking around the room dramatically before finishing,"-were it's eyes. They were violet."

I felt my face do that weird thing when you find out something that was totally unexpected. It scrunched up and my mouth turned down into a frown and my eyes widened. She paid no attention to me, continuing the story. "And then the wolf spoke to her, in her mind. She was greatly troubled at first, but soon came to realize that this White Wolf meant no harm. So she asked him why he visited her. And he responded," Do you not know who I am?" The Queen, now afraid, nodded, even though she did not. All she had to do was politely say no, but she didn't. And now she just lied to the White Wolf, which would undoubtedly go unpunished. He knew this, and became angry. So he cursed her."

Everyone was leaning forward in their seats, even though I'm sure they've already heard it a million times before. I held my breath as I waited for her to finish. I was almost positive that the White Wolf she was talking about was the same one I healed. It had to be.

"The curse was this: You will not be able to bear children." It was here she paused the story to add her own comment. "Such a common curse, yet very devastating, especially for the Queen who was expected to bring forth an heir to the throne. So she pleaded, she begged, some say she even fell to the ground on her knees. But this is what she said. "Please, anything else. I did not know who you were, do not curse me just because of my foolish ways!"

"And this greatly pleased the White Wolf, for she had seen that she was wrong and asked forgiveness. So he instead placed upon her a blessing. 'May all those of the female in your family line obtain the gift of healing. With just a exhale of air upon the wounded and weak, and they will be restored to their full health."

"And so it was. The Queen gave the King two sons and a daughter. The daughter had the gift of healing, and her daughter, and so on. About 1,000 years ago, one of the females from the family line did not have a girl. She was heartbroken, but then the Moon Goddess appeared to her and made a deal. She would grant the woman the ability to have a girl if her family line became werewolves, who were well known back then and were greatly admired. And the woman of course agreed and bore a baby girl that she name Lilia. That was the last we have seen or heard of from the Queen's lineage."

Her eyes zeroed in on me. "Until you."

As she continued talking, she started walking towards me in slow steps. "We thought the lineage was lost, but you are proof that we were wrong and you indeed are still very much alive. That is why we call you the Lost Hybrid. Once lost, but now you are found in all your glory."

I fought the urge to raise an eyebrow. So she was a little much, with the theatrics and all, but she seemed nice enough. I had to find out who the 'we' was that she kept referring to.

"And who is 'we?'" I asked, twisting in my seat to face her when she came up behind me.

"The Hybrid Pack. Yes, that is our name." She said when she saw me ready to ask another question. "We know all of this about you're family because the White Wolf has visited one of us and told us to find you."

I bit my lip before asking," Does the Myth have a name?"

"Rhaknorisk."

So did that mean my mom knew about all of this and even had the same healing abilities as me? She told me about Rhaknorisk, but not in so much detail. And if she knew what I could do, why did she want to hide it?

Thoughts about my mom lead me to thoughts about our last moments together, which then led me to think about Phoenix. Was he looking for me? He said he would, but we didn't know each other very well, and I wasn't very nice to him.

He's our mate of course he's looking for you. My wolf huffed in annoyance and I answered,' How do you know? Maybe he decided I was perfectly fine all the way where ever I am-'

That was when I realized that I knew my background and history, found out some things about myself that I never thought would be uncovered, had someone make an oath to the Moon Goddess that they wouldn't hurt me, but I still didn't know where I was.

"Where am I?" I asked the woman, and she gave a nod to everyone sitting around the table. They all got up and exited out a side door, giving us much needed privacy. I noticed with relief that even Naomi and Alexander left.

"You're still in England."

I gave an involuntary sigh of relief and she smiled softly. "We are also making plans to get into contact with Alpha Phoenix."

I sat up straight, then decided to heck with sitting up straight. I stood up and faced her, my palms resting on the back of the chair. "I want to talk to him right now. I want to explain everything that has happened to me-"

"I'm afraid you can't do that." She interjected, and I tilted my head, which was a sign that I was about to get very mad very quick.

"And I'm afraid that you're not able to tell me what I can or can't do. If I want to call him, I will. Am I a prisoner?" As I spoke, my voice got quieter and quieter, until by the end it was so low that I knew she was only able to hear me because of her werewolf hearing.

"You are by no means a prisoner, Lost Hybrid-"

"My name is Adira." I snapped, frustrated. How had this turned downhill so quickly?

"I apologize. You aren't a prisoner, Adira." She said just as quietly as me, emphasizing my name. "But you were taken here by force and that should tell you your place."

I bared my teeth. "My place? I am the Lost Hybrid, as you keep reminding me. I would think that holds some sort of power. I will call my mate and explain things whether you want me to or not!"

All she did was sadly look in the distance out a nearby window. "Don't say I didn't warn you." She said in the same tone she's been using the entire time we've been talking. She reached inside her back pocket and produced a phone.

I grabbed it and realized I didn't have his number memorized. He had taken my phone and put his number in my contacts (and also deleted all my contacts who were guys, but that's beside the point), so if I could get back my phone then everything would be sorted out.

I told her as much and she turned a palm upward. "Then I don't know. But you should ask Alexander, he was the one that took your belongings and put them somewhere."

I took a deep breath to calm myself down. "Thank you for finally explaining to me who I am. I truly am grateful for that, but I do not like being told I cannot have contact with my mate. Sure, you warned me. Okay then, I will remember that. Now, do you know where I could find Alexander?"

The woman's lips turned downward. "No, I do not take it upon myself to know where he is at all times."

I sensed the bitter sarcasm but made no further comment. Instead, I gave a terse nod and left, in search of Alexander. Luckily, I paid attention to where they took me and knew where in the house I was. The room I woke up in was upstairs, two doors down to the left, so I decided it would be smart to start there. My instincts must have been right because I saw him in there. He was smoothing down some of the sheets on the bed, and I strolled over there.

"Got house cleaning duty?" I casually said, and he jumped about 5 feet in the air. He spun around, a hand over his heart.

"Jesus, Adira, didn't your mother ever tell you it was impolite to sneak up on people?"

I shrugged, acting passive aggressive. There was a small bandage on my throat from where he cut me, and it stung every now and then. I found it embarrassing I didn't heal quickly like other werewolves, and my wound not healing drew even more attention to me than was necessary.

He seemed to know because he rubbed the back of his neck. "Look, I'm sorry. I was too rough, I know. Just hoping you'll not stay mad at me?"

When I didn't answer but he saw my almost smile, he was motivated to keep talking, and even joked around. "Please, I don't want a beautiful girl like you mad at me, it would ruin my ladies man reputation."

This time I couldn't hold in the snort and he burst out laughing. When he finally calmed down, wiping his eyes, I held out a hand. "I need my phone."

Instantly he sobered. "Sorry, sweet cheeks, but I don't think that's possible."

"That woman said I could." For the first time, I realized I didn't know the name of the one who shed light on my situation. Alexander offered," Ms. Rosey? The one who was in charge of the meeting?"

When I nodded, he sighed and took my phone out of his pocket. Before he handed it to me, he asked," Who are you calling?"

"Phoenix." I responded without pausing, and he winced but agreed to let me do that.

"Ok, sure. And what are you going to tell him?"

I hesitated. Should I tell him where I was? Well, all I knew was that I was still in England, but not my exact location. I would just tell him everything I found out, and then see what he says.

I told this to Alexander and he grudgingly handed the phone over. When I was just about to press 'call Phoenix' and I realized Alexander still hadn't left the room, I made shooing motions with my hands and his head fell back and he left in long, slow strides, dramatically slugging forward. When he was out of the room, I rushed to the door and closed and locked it, then called Alpha Phoenix.

The phone didn't even ring one time before he answered. "Adira, are you there?" He didn't even give me a full second to respond before he yelled," Adira!"

"I'm here, I'm here!" I said quickly, relieved to hear his voice.

I heard his shaky intake of breath. "God, Adira are you okay? Please tell me your okay, fuck, when I see who took you I will fucking rip their heads off-"

"No, Phoenix, please." I interrupted him, and he quieted. "I'm okay."

"Someone kidnapped you, majesty, and I don't know where you are. You cannot just call me days later and expect me to believe you when you say 'I'm okay.'"

"Have you heard of the legend Rhaknorisk?" I asked him, focusing on the task at hand.

I heard him hesitate through the phone and that was all I needed to know. Just before I was about to tell him everything, the door slammed open and what I saw made me weak.

It was The White Wolf.

CHAPTER 12

The White Wolf was quite the sight to behold, and I didn't mean in a good way. His fur was matted with dried blood, and fresh blood still dripped from his body onto the floor. His muzzle was surrounded by dark red liquid and his eyes had a fierce gleam in them.

I gasped, sickened at the thought that someone would do this to him. Maybe I could heal him like I did before-

"Their coming." He managed to mindlink me before he fell to the ground. I yelped and ran over to him to find that he wasn't there. He had just...vanished.

My eyes widened and I looked around the room, searching for any sign that what just happened actually happened and I wasn't going crazy. Then, I saw a small blood smudge on the doorway and felt oddly relieved. I wasn't losing my mind.

The door banged open again and I got into attack mode, crouching low to the ground and ready to shift. It was Alexander, and his eyes were wild with something I never thought they would be full of: Fear.

"Grab your phone and bag, we're leaving right now." He demanded, and when he turned to go I ran to him and grabbed his arm. He whipped around and glared at me. "I don't have time for this. Someone dangerous is coming and we need to leave now."

With that said, he yanked out of my now weak grasp and left me gaping after him. I didn't have time to dwell on my hurt feelings, and instead grabbed my phone which I had dropped on the floor. The screen was completely cracked, and shattered fragments fell off as I gently picked it up. I knew it was hopeless but still tried to power it on.

Nothing.

I shouted in frustration. No! How would Phoenix know I was safe?

You don't even know yourself yet if you're safe, My wolf said to me, and I growled but packed up my things. I took the phone even though it was broken and stashed it away in my bag. I heard the pounding of feet right outside my door and yanked it open, the force causing it to rip of its hinges. I stared at the broken door but Alex rushed past me and my shocked figure. "It doesn't matter. Now follow me and try not to get killed!"

I wore my bag as a backpack and ran after him, my feet pounding on the hardwood floors. We made it to the balcony overlooking the first floor, the one right next to the stair banister. He cursed as soon as he saw what was taking place in the house.

Wolves of all shapes and sizes were fighting below us, snarls and screams filling the air. "How did this happen?" I shouted over the noise. "How did they get in, I thought the security was tight-"

"It is! I'm not sure what happened but we need to find Ms. Rosey this instant." He shot back and then said," Stay here, I'll be right back."

Before I could protest, he left, leaving me looking at his retreating figure. This was my chance, a perfect opportunity to leave and never come back. I could try to find Phoenix...but how realistic was that? I didn't know where he was or what else was outside these borders. For wolf's sake I didn't even know where I was! I would play it safe and stay with this pack until I was sure of my plan.

Another yelp brought me back to the present and my gaze became determined as I looked down at the massacre happening below. These people may have kidnapped me but it was with good intentions: they finally explained my abilities and how I came to be, and brought me out of the dark. I'd be damned if I just stood around and did nothing.

I had to help.

I saw a flash of blond hair, and when I looked more closely I realized it was Alexander. I saw another wolf creep up behind him, about to pounce. I opened my mouth to yell a warning, but someone else beat me to it.

Naomi. She ran past me and down the stairs, shouting at the wolf to gain it's attention. "Fight me. Mutt! Come on, the only reason you won't is because you know you'll lose!"

That got the wolf's attention. The wolf turned around, ignoring Alexander, and pounced on Naomi before she could shift. The last thing I saw before she was mauled was her serene expression, like a sort of peace came over her. It was clear she mindlinked something to Alexander, who fought the wolves left to right with a ferocity I didn't know he owned. He howled in anger as Naomi fell to the ground, lifeless, with the wolf tearing into her body.

I joined in yelling with rage. She had tended to my wound, had been a friend for a day. And now she was gone. All I saw was red.

I shifted, and though my small wolf could be underestimated, I had speed and fierce determination on my side.

I charged the wolf that had killed Naomi, and before it even had time to react, I closed my jaws around it's throat and twisted my head from side to side. It yelped in pain but I didn't let go, not until it was limp in my jaws. I felt the presence of another wolf about to attack me and so I dropped the one I killed without remorse, then spun around and attacked the brown one creeping up behind me. That was a clean and quick kill, all I did was snap its neck.

I did this for I don't know how long, but I was definitely slowing down. It seemed the wolves were endless. It seemed we weren't even making a dent in whichever pack decided to attack us.

All of a sudden, my senses were sent into overdrive. I smelled cinnamon and...was that cotton candy? In my distraction, one of the enemy decided to use this to his advantage. I felt a sharp, awful pain in my left leg. On instinct, I growled and spun around, ready to attack.

There was a huge grey wolf right behind me, with blood dripping down it's snout and muzzle and a growl ripping past it's sharp teeth. It sprang at me, but I was ready. I grabbed its throat in my mouth but before I could do any real damage, she was abruptly yanked away from me.

If I thought the grey wolf was huge, then I was sorely mistaken. The wolf that had taken her off of me was a male, and towered over me. His coat was a shiny midnight black, eerily similar to Phoenix's. He was also the source of the smell.

His eyes were a mix between dark blue and purple, and the mix of the two colors were beautiful. I could stare at them for ages and never look away-

He growled, bringing me back to the present. What the hell was I doing? I had only ever lost my train of thought and sense when I had met my-

The black wolf shifted back into his human form and growled, "Mate."

CHAPTER 13

I wanted to avert my eyes, but also wanted to keep an eye on the enemy. What I chose to do was keep my eyes on his face and never look below his chest.

"Everyone out!" He yelled, then proceeded to yell something else in another language, one I didn't recognize. The other language sounded old, ancient.

"Mate." The man in front of me growled again once everyone from his pack was out. "Shift."

Though he gave off the aurora of an Alpha, I refused to do anything this murderer told me to. In fact, I would do the exact opposite. I sensed the others from the Hybrid pack form a protection barrier behind me, and some flanked me. I noticed one of those that flanked me was Alexander, and he gave me a nod of encouragement, letting me know he was right beside me.

A human girl, small, approached me with a short pink towel, presumably to cover myself with if I chose to shift. I tilted my head at her and snagged the towel in my jaws.

I stared at the man in front of me. He clenched his jaw in anger. I had to admit, he was beyond handsome. He looked eerily like Phoenix, except more...how to put this? Dangerous. His dark hair was close cut on the edges and longer in the front, and his complexion was darker, more tan than Phoenix's. His face was also more angular, sculpted. Where Phoenix was handsome no doubt, he was more of a pretty boy. The man in front of me was, simply put, a sex god.

I noticed his hands clench at his sides, and I rolled my eyes as much as I could in wolf form before shifting. Quickly, I wrapped the towel around myself and hoped I wouldn't regret my decision. I knew this made me slightly weak as I was now in my human form, but I could shift extremely fast, another one of my skills.

"That's not possible." I spoke with confidence, looking him in the eye. I would not let him belittle me.

He smirked, crossing his arms over his chest, and whether intentional or not, flexing. "Oh, but it is. I'm guessing you've already met Nix?"

A beat of silence passed. He couldn't possibly mean Phoenix-?

"Alpha Phoenix?" I asked, just in case.

All he had to do was tilt his head to confirm my worst suspicions. Phoenix had lied to me. He told me there wasn't any secrets that would affect me permanently, and I was a fool and trusted him. But first, I had to make sure the man in front of me was telling the truth.

"How do I know you're telling the truth?" I made sure my voice was strong and the tears weren't in my eyes. There would be time for that later. But right now, the pack that had helped me know who I truly was was in serious danger, and I needed to tread carefully.

"Call him. Ask him." He replied as if it was nothing.

"I don't have a working phone or know his number." I couldn't believe I was actually contemplating this. This man had to be lying.

"Then use mine." He whistled, and a wolf from his pack entered the door and ran towards us. Immediately everyone around me growled, but their leader raised a hand. "He's giving me clothes to cover, and my phone for Adira. That is all."

Though they stopped growling, they still were on full alert and their teeth were bared.

He put shorts on, and then reached in the back pocket and produced a phone. "You can call him on this. He will answer, I assure you this."

I stepped forward two spaces and snatched the phone out of his rough hand. I backed up and looked at the phone to see it already had his number plugged in. All I had to do was press call. So I did.

One ring, two rings three rin-

"Adira." He breathed, sounding panicked.

"Is it true?" I asked, my voice harsh. "Do you have a twin brother?"

I sensed rather than heard him tense. When he replied, his voice was pleading. "Please, majesty, let me explain."

"No. I'm not doing this here, in front of everyone. Your brother is going to take me to you, and then we are all going to have a nice, long chat."

I hung up on his protests and pocketed the phone. I then focused my attention on the Alpha in front of me, who also was supposedly my mate. "What is your name?"

"Alpha Daire." He answered immediately, and the second he said that, growls erupted from the throats of the wolves surrounding me.

I was at a loss. "What is it?"

Alexander shifted and quickly put on shorts before grabbing my elbow and whispering in my ear," Ask to talk about this. He'll grant you permission, he has no choice."

Alpha Daire snarled, and I glared at him. "Chill out. I want to talk this over with Alex.""No." Came his instant reply. What was it with these boys? Always growling and bossing me around, deciding I wasn't able to talk to anyone else other than them!

"Yes. 10 minutes, that's all I ask, Daire." I said his name on purpose, hoping it would emit a response. I wasn't disappointed. His eyes darkened and he clenched his jaw but gave a terse nod.

I wasn't taking any second chances, so I let Alex lead me to the room upstairs. The second the door closed, he whisper yelled," Did you know about this? Did you? TELL ME!" He fired at me without time to reply, and after his last outburst, he slammed me against the wall.

I tried to calm him down. "Alex, I didn't know, I swear on the Moon Goddess!"

It seemed to do the trick because he sighed and let go of me. He turned his face away from me, but I saw the tear trailing down his cheek. "Almost half the pack, Adira. At the hands of that monster." He spat with disgust.

I balled my hands into fists and felt like screaming. I wondered how it was fair that this fate should be mine. I just wished I had a normal, possibly Beta mate who was sweet and kind. However, I knew it was futile to dream about something that wouldn't come true. Instead, I had to focus on what I could do to make the situation more bearable.

"I have to go with him. It's the only way you guys will be safe."

Even before I was done, he was shaking his head. "No. You'll be in danger-"

"So will you guys! Half your pack is gone, Alex! Nobody else can die because of me."

As I said it, I knew that what had happened here today was my fault. The thought almost brought me to my knees, but luckily Alex was there to hold me steady. "Adira? You alright?"

He made a move to pick me up and set me on the bed, with only pure intentions I'm sure, but I knocked his hands away. "No. I mean, yes, I'm fine. Look, if this in any way can make up for what happened, I've got to take it."

Alex looked me dead in the eye with a serious expression. "What the hell are you talking about?"

I struggled to keep the tears away and stay strong. When I spoke, there was a catch in my throat but I managed to get through it. "This is all my fault. He came here because of me, he killed your pack members because of me...Alex, I don't think I will ever be able to make up for that, but let me start with leading him away from you and the Hybrid pack. It's the least I can do with everything you did for me."

Before he could protest, I grabbed the duffel bag hanging on the door, threw some clothes inside and changed, not caring that he saw because I was leaving anyway. I heard him gasp when he saw the scars littering my back, but I was too preoccupied to truly notice. I rushed out the bedroom door and down the stairs, my bag in a tight grip. I stopped right in front of Alpha Daire and firmly said," We're leaving now."

He grinned, a grin that contained darkness and irresistible charm all in one. "Let's go."

EPILOGUE

I refused to talk to him, to acknowledge him, to even look in his direction. This wasn't how things were supposed to turn out. However, I was an Alpha's daughter and had to take matter into my own hands. Even if the situation I was in wasn't ideal, I had to turn the table so matters rested in my hands, and my hands only.

We were in his car, a limited edition Bugatti Veyron. He had made sure to tell me, but all I did was get in the back and slam the door. He sighed but got the message, climbing into the driver's seat.

30 minutes have passed, and apparently, he couldn't take it anymore because he said," You know, I'm really not a bad guy."

And though it was true I had stayed silent all this time, I couldn't help but snap back," Tell that to the ones you slaughtered."

Through the seats, I saw his hands clench the steering wheel and smiled. Good. He should be angry, though mostly at himself for what he did. Alpha Daire slightly turned his head in my direction when he next addressed me. "Look, I had to find you-"

"And that involved killing half of a pack? Please. Save it for someone who cares." I wasn't having any of it. Just because he was my mate didn't mean I wanted him. Or anything to do with him.

Ok, maybe I was taking it too far in taunting him, and even I knew he didn't have enough patience to not correct me and show me' I'm an Alpha and you have to submit to me and blahbidy blah.'

Sure enough, he yanked the steering wheel to the left and parked us haphazardly on the side of the road. We were alone, with nothing but straight open road and trees sur-rounding us. His breathing was heavy, and when he turned to look at me his eyes were completely black. That either meant he was aroused or angry, and I'm sure he wasn't aroused. He was an Alpha. He didn't like having someone disrespect him, whether it was in front of company or not. It was just that way with Alphas. You could never predict what they were going to say or do next.

I would know, being the Alpha's daughter. With my mind thinking about that, about my Dad and his eyes turning black, I started to relive what my father had done to me a few years ago. Like every time this happened, I tried to think about something else, anything else, but it was too late.

I was in his office, in front of his wooden desk. He was sitting in the chair, his muscles tense. When he spoke to me, his voice was furious. "What did I tell you, Adira?"

I tried to defend myself. "He was harassing and touching me and I had to fight back-"

"He is the son of one of the most powerful Alpha's!" He yelled, turning around and standing up.

I refused to back down. "So, for your reputation, you wanted me to just stand there and take it? He had that punch coming to him."

My Dad shook his head at me. "Adira, I told you to play nice. I told you to get to know him, to be his friend. For God's sake, I wanted you two to marry! That's what I wanted. It would have been a perfect deal. You and him married, and I join forces with one of the most powerful Alpha's. Why couldn't you have at least pretended to like him, for the sake of your father?"

"You know I love you, but I refuse to be a pawn in your game. What you're suggesting is sick, cruel. He's 46 years old, Dad! I'm not going to bloody marry him!" I yelled, my hands in a fist.

That was when the first strike came. He picked up a glass vase from his desk and hurled it at me. His eyes were completely black, and I knew his wolf had taken over. I needed to get out of there, fast. Or else my life could be in serious danger.

The vase was so fast, I only had time to turn around before it shattered, the pieces ripping into my back. I let out a breath of pain and raised my hands. "Dad, just listen to me!"

He growled in rage and threw another, then another. Four more shattered vases cutting my skin, and his eyes returned to their normal color. Every time I tried to leave, he would manage to aim so the glass would hit my back. When he finally had control over his mind and body again and saw what he did to me, he let out a choked cry. "Baby girl, I am so sorry...Please, believe me."

He reached out to me but I shook my head.

"You stay the hell away from me." I managed, then turned and ran out the door.

"...Adira! Adira, baby, listen to me. You're alright, you're here. I'm here."

The first thing I noticed when I came to was that I wasn't in the front seat anymore. I was in the backseat, laying across someone's legs and I felt a cool hand stroking my hair off my forehead.

"Shhh. You're right here, I'm with you. I've got you, baby."

I let out a soft sigh, still not really aware of what was going on. These memory attacks had been getting more frequent lately, and I wasn't sure what triggered them. I didn't even know it was possible until I started having them. Like I always did when I tried to get back to reality, I counted by 6's. 6, 12, 18, 24..

I got to 72 when I fully realized exactly what situation I was in. Fuck. Daire was hovering above me, and I was laying across his lap. His hands were holding my head, supporting me, and I could feel my face was wet with tears. I wasn't sure what happened during the time I was reliving awful memories, but I think I freaked out and yelled some things because he kept murmuring," You can calm down now. You're okay, Shhhh. No more talking, I've got you."

I bolted upright, and he barely moved his head out of the way to avoid getting a broken nose.

"Adira!" He yelled when I stumbled out of the car. This was too much.

Apparently I had two mates, one of who pretended to be a dick but said he was just acting, and another who was the twin and killed half of the pack that helped me know who I really was, I found out my mother was lying to me my whole life, my memory attacks had been getting more and more frequent and I wasn't sure I could take it much longer. Everything was a mess, and I had been so strong up until this point.

I hugged my arms to my chest and put one foot in front of the other, away from Alpha Daire and my problems and responsibilities.

"Adira! Come back!" Daire yelled, and I heard him running to catch up to me.

I shook my head. No, I couldn't do this. When I felt his breath on the back of my neck, I panicked and started sprinting away. I don't think he realized how fast I was because he cursed before chasing after me. "Fuck."

After a few minutes, I thought I lost him but then he dropped down right in front of me.

I tried to backpedal, but he easily caught up to me. I tried to swerve around him but he grabbed me in his arms and hugged me to his chest. I tried to fight him. "Get off me! I hate you, get off of me! Let me go!" I screamed, punching him in the chest.

He didn't say anything, just pulled me closer.

I beat my fists against him, twisting in his hold and yelling.

I didn't realize I was sobbing until I settled down enough to hear my own cries. I felt the wetness on my cheeks and all of a sudden, my legs couldn't support my own weight anymore. My eyes fluttered and I let go of his shirt, crumbling.

"Adira." Daire looked into my eyes, worry etched on his beautiful face.

"I'm..I can't stay..." Is all I managed before I passed out for the second time that day.

I wasn't sure if it was the trauma of seeing all of those dead werewolves, or my flashback session, or just the knowledge of another mate. It was probably all three of those and the fact that I wasn't strong enough to handle it. The Moon Goddess made a mistake when she picked these mates for me, and when she decided I was to be the Lost Hybrid.

I was too weak.